Korvu:
The Beginning

A prequel to THE WILD ONE

by

MARGARET GREGORY

TAT Publishing

Also by Margaret Gregory

TYMOREAN TRUST SERIES:
Book 1 - Power Rising
Book 2 - Great Ones
Book 3 - The Return to Earth
Book 4 – Earth Mission
Book 5 – Alien Contact

ATAPI SORCERESS SERIES:
Book 1- The Wild One
Book 2 – Atapi Sorceress

THE THIRD GENERATION SERIES
Wanda: From Bad to Worse
Wanda: Choosing Crime

Cover designed by msgdragon

Cover Image Credit:
© Can Stock Photo Inc. / Nejron

For permission requests, address the request to the author c/o
Permissions,
TAT Publishing
PO Box 150
Glen Waverly, Vic. 3150
Australia
www.tatpublishing.com

Korvu - The Beginning

Chapter 1

The old female sighed but waited until Stacion Ansuni stalked off with his youngest boy child, heading for his cave. Only then did she rise from her squatting position, stretch carefully and begin her slow walk across the cleared village centre to the girl child still curled into a ball of misery.

Even though her legs were growing stiffer and her wing stubs ached – the pain meant that she still lived. Her hair might be as white as the clouds but her mind was as sharp as ever. Her heart was still strong enough and big enough to love the discarded girl-child that Stacion Ansuni had kicked aside.

"Come to Mama Okuta, Jai-warrior," she said gently, lifting the little girl from the dusty ground and hugging her. The girl's smooth brown-skinned arms reached around her neck.

Mama Okuta could feel the misery emanating from the child who stayed quiet even though her desire to howl was so strong. Beneath that, she felt power stirring. It flowed from the girl-child and the pain and stiffness went away.

"Holy Mother Larcia," Mama Okuta breathed. "Thank you, Jai-warrior."

"Mama Okuta, you are the only one who hugs me. I didn't want it to hurt you," the quiet voice spoke. The misery had receded. Now the dominant emotion was smug satisfaction.

"How did you know how to do what you did, little one?"

"My brother told me," Jai Ansuni said very quietly. "He will be a sorcerer, but father said I had no magic and I was no whelp of his."

Mama Okuta nodded in understanding. "Would you like to learn more?"

Jai Ansuni nodded. "Sorcery?"

"Of a kind. Women's magic. Something that is secret from the men."

Jai giggled softly. "Yes." Her answer was definite.

"Then I will petition the tribal council to adopt you," Mama Okuta promised. "I will say that I need young hands to help me now that I am old."

"Are you old, Mama?" Jai asked.

"I am old enough to remember your sire's predecessor," she said with pride. She did not say that he had been a much better sorcerer devil than his whelp Stacion. Or that it had been an ill-day when Mastro Ansuni had failed to win against Stacion's challenge.

"And yes, I'm old. Look at how my skin is dry and mottled. Yours is strong, with a faint lustre."

Jai looked at her brown skin and at Mama Okuta's. Once again, power began to flow.

"Nay, Jai-warrior," Mama Okuta put her hand on the little girl's hand. "As I am serves me well enough. Save your power for now. We use it in the secret women's rituals. It would not do for males to see it being used."

The little girl nodded solemnly. She suddenly seemed so much wiser than her five summers.

Chapter 2 - Eleven years on

"That way is so much easier," Con Ansuni commented as he squatted next to his sister. They were in the cave he had been given to denote his rank as apprentice sorcerer.

"How did you do that? Father's ritual to create glowing rocks takes hours."

"Women's magic," Jai told him. She shared all she learnt from the women with him. He would not betray her. Nor would she ever reveal that Con was teaching her 'men's' magic because that was forbidden and neither of them would ever admit that they could each hear the thoughts of their womb-mate.

"Does it really take that long? I can't see why?" Jai said.

"Perhaps to teach me patience," Con muttered. "I'll never be good enough for him."

"You and I are not so different then," Jai spoke flatly, revealing the long entrenched resentment. She suddenly tensed, glancing out of the cave entrance.

"Oh, damn! Siluci Danka is coming."

Jai stood up and looked around the cave to ensure no signs of their magic working remained.

Con didn't doubt his sister, even though he couldn't see Siluci yet.

"I'm out of here," Con said quickly. "She may be father's latest favourite, but I really detest her."

"Why don't you try that other magic I taught you," was Jai's sly suggestion. "She's been ogling you a lot these past two days. If she's looking for you, you'll see how well she can see."

Con chuckled and allowed himself to sink into the aura of Korvu. To Jai's eyes, he disappeared but she sensed him near the entrance. She grinned to let Con know he had succeeded. This was a magic that Stacion had not even hinted at. Con wondered if he was aware it was possible.

"What are you doing here, freak-born?" Siluci Danka demanded as she arrived, looking around Con's cave. She peeked behind the privacy curtain as Jai was using a reed broom to remove blown in leaves.

"I was sent here to clean up," Jai lied, infusing her answer with feigned resentment. "It seems that I am useful for drudging for my brother."

"Half-brother," Siluci corrected, parroting the 'truth' that Stacion claimed.

Jai didn't need to see the malicious smile on the other girl's face.

"I heard them say that you are with egg. Congratulations," she said without enthusiasm. Such disinterest was a sure way to get Siluci to talk. Jai wanted to know what she was doing coming to Con's cave.

"Yes, the sorcerer has given me a child," Siluci preened.

Jai sensed the other girl's fear and that let her hear Siluci's thoughts. She had just been told that it wasn't true. That the bleeding she had noticed meant that she had aborted the egg. She was afraid that Stacion would be angry with her and she would lose her privileged status. She was so afraid that she had concocted a draught of teki weed to induce her fertility cycle. She was now out to seduce Con.

"I can almost feel sorry for her," Jai said mentally to the nearby Con, after sharing what she had sensed.

"I might risk it," Con considered. "If she is that desperate, she'll owe me favours."

"She is also the most malicious gossip in the tribe," Jai warned him. "Do you trust her to keep her mouth shut?"

"I dare say self-preservation will do that," Con commented. "Though why me?"

"Because father would know if the child didn't have his blood," Jai told him.

"But you – and I – he said…" Con disagreed.

"He knew," Jai thought resentfully. "He didn't want a girl-child – it lowered his maleness. So he concocted that tale of Mother lying with two males – so he had an excuse to kill her and disregard me."

"But…"

"Brother, once a woman has conceived an egg – she can lie with whomever and they won't start another egg. It's impossible."

"Should I do this?" Con asked. He wasn't unwilling but he valued his sister's instincts.

"If you want," Jai said, continuing to sweep the dirt floor of the cave and still ignoring Siluci.

"As obnoxious as she is, I don't think she deserves to be punished for a perfectly natural occurrence. Besides, I like the idea of you outsmarting Him. He'll be away a few days while Lancho is being tested at the Rock. Just find a way to seal her mouth. I don't want to lose you."

Jai proceeded to improve Con's bed into a comfortable nest by shaking out the ferns and placing the hare's wool rug over them. She was aware that Siluci was glaring at her.

"Out of here, freak born," the girl said.

Jai was used to the taunt and ignored it. "Be careful that you don't create a freak-born of your own. Or don't you remember what your mate did to my mother?"

It was obvious that she did know. "I won't be so stupid," was her retort.

Jai hid her smile as she left the cave. Siluci really was ignorant. She believed Stacion's lie, just because he, as the tribe's Devil had said it was so. The elder women knew better, and they had taught the truth to Jai Ansuni. It was just better not to openly disagree and now too late to matter. For the tribes greater good it had to be that way. The tribe needed warriors and it also needed strong females to breed warriors.

The only reason that Siluci was daring to cheat on her mate was that her first egg had already aborted. If Con conceived another on her – she could tell the healers they were wrong. And probably the Elder women would say nothing. They would know though.

Time would tell if, after all the trouble, she whelped a girl.

Chapter 3

"Lancho, I said you could choose a female from the unmated cavern," Stacion Ansuni stated. His manner was touched with well controlled anger. He stared at his elder son as if his son was not forcing a female into a mating posture and as if there was no female there.

Lancho, confused and aroused and full of fermented hare's milk, backed away from the female he had chosen. He sensed his sire's anger, but was slow to guess the reason.

He was, however, smart enough to obey the implied instruction, without comment, and to flee his cave.

Stacion continued to stare across the cave as if no one was there.

Jai collected her loin cloth and waist bag and straightened up as she pulled her tunic down. She glanced at the profile of her sire and walked out. She kept her bearing erect and her chin up. Larcia help any woman Lancho picked next, she thought. She was grateful for her sire's interruption, even though it wasn't from any particular concern for her.

Still, the arrogant egomaniac had saved her from Lancho's rough handling. In spite of his claims to the contrary, he knew she was his whelp. And, in spite of all the things he did that endangered the tribe – he wouldn't weaken the tribe by breeding within his bloodline. After all the years, sixteen of them, it was recognition of sorts.

Jai went to the river to wash away her half-brother's touch – and considered the knowledge she had gained from Lancho's mind.

The privilege of mating had not been a reward for him, but a consolation. He had sat through the night vigil at the Rock of Arkor, with the other senior apprentice devils, but of all of them, only he had not received his secret name.

Jai savoured the realisation that both Lancho and her sire had lost face. She doubted that Lancho would ever get his secret name. He was mentally warped. He delighted in torturing and killing for its own sake. Her father at least created feasible justification for his deeds. In all ways, Lancho was worse than her father.

Stacion had stated that Lancho would try again in the next season – he was the youngest aspirant there. Feasible, but Jai preferred to believe that the aura of Korvu knew that if he had the power over a tribe he would bring them to ruin.

Jai allowed herself to drift down the river with the current until the river widened into a lake. The warm sun shone onto the water and made her feel too exposed. She swam to the shallows and took shelter amongst some overhanging trees. It was quiet there – and peaceful. Her conscience did not bother her for avoiding the women's duties. No one would come looking for her – they never did. The only time she was set work was when she was with the other unmated females of mating age. Then, she was just another of the crowd. Alone, no one acknowledged her – at least not in the open, but in the women's places, she was known and respected for her healing skills.

This time alone, sitting in the shallow water, restored her self-esteem. She felt the aura of Korvu, filling her with power.

The water in this little inlet was still and she could see her reflection in it. She let her long black hair out of its loose braid and ducked under the water. When she surfaced and allowed the water to grow still again, she saw it slicked to her head and neck.

She used the still water as a mirror and braided her hair again so it stayed away from her face.

The sound of galloping hooves disturbed her meditation and made her draw deeper into the shadows. The sound preceded the group who came into her view through a gap in the leaves and stopped on the far side of the lake.

As the riders dismounted, Jai studied the animals. She had never seen anything like them before. She watched the powerful muscles rippling under their pelt and the grace with which they walked. She admired the way they lowered their proud necks to drink and flicked their tails to brush away flies.

The animals were so beautiful that for a long time she ignored the riders. When she noticed them her guts seemed to tighten. All were pale skinned, pale haired humanoids. Although she had never seen any before, she knew what they were – Kumatan. She had learnt as a small child that the Kumatan hunted Atapi and killed or enslaved her people – treated them like animals. They had Traegers – slave masters – who could negate even the power of the sorcerer devils, though Stacion loudly declaimed that he was stronger than any Traeger that had ever lived.

Jai stayed into the shadows and felt the aura of Korvu hiding her from any chance glance of the Kumatan. If they saw her, they would know what she was by her brown skin and round face. She should slip away and warn the tribe, but fascination held her there. Stacion, no doubt would sense the Kumatan soon enough. Meanwhile, she would learn what she could of her people's enemy.

This group did not seem like a hunting party or a war party. They seemed ignorant of the fact that they were so close to her tribe's territory. The river was the boundary, and at this point so was the lake. That was why Jai liked it here; it was as far as she could go from the village yet still be in the tribe's territory. Crossing the river, leaving their territory was not only forbidden, it was dangerous.

Jai heard the voices from the group and their tone was relaxed. She looked closer at the riders and saw two who were shorter than the rest. One of those was dressed differently, wearing a flowing garment, not a tunic and leg coverings. Jai was sure that she was seeing a girl of the Kumatan. That idea intrigued her. She would like to meet that girl, but would she be like the males and think her an animal?

Jai sensed a disturbance in the aura. Her father was coming with his warriors. She sensed his anger and his bloodlust.

"No!" her mind rebelled. "Go away," she yelled silently. "Flee!"

It seemed that her mental yell had been heard and she shrunk further into the aura. Terse orders were given and all the riders quickly remounted and galloped their beasts away.

Jai saw her sire run into her sight on the tribe's side of the lake. He incanted a spell to warp the water out of his way and allow him and his warriors could run across the lake bed.

When he was on the other side she heard him bellow with rage. One of the warriors picked up a glittering object and gave it to Stacion. He studied it, growled and gestured his warriors onward following the tracks of the animals.

Stacion turned slowly around, staring at everything his eyes saw. His sight passed over Jai's hiding place and his spell of seeking slithered around her without revealing her.

Jai slunk lower into the water and the aura. He had heard her warning. The knowledge sobered her. She had used a sorcerer's power to project her thought. He was alert now, but he would not think it was her, but some young male from another tribe, encroaching on his territory. Finally, he turned and followed his warriors.

Jai raised herself so her body floated on the water. The movement brought a sudden surge of power. Stacion had trapped the water. It caused her to be rolled under and feeling her lungs fill with water, she panicked, calling to Larcia for help. Her mind filled with the sense of fish and she felt her arms become more flexible. Her last coherent thought was to flee.

Finally, the sense of her own shape filled her mind and she felt her own shape returning. Her feet touched the pebbly bottom of the river and she stood up and walked to the bank where she had entered, hours ago.

"Who taught you to change shape?"

The voice startled her and she spun around. She breathed easier moments later when she saw her brother emerge from the cover of some trees and that he was alone.

"What?"

"You were a fish. You changed shape. Father hasn't taught me how to do that yet."

Jai glanced over her shoulder in the direction of the lake. "It must be instinctive. I was in danger. Why are you here?"

"Father has gone off chasing Kumatan. I knew you had come this way and felt your fear," Con admitted. "I'm glad they didn't hurt you."

"They didn't cross the river," Jai told him. "They were riding the most marvellous creatures…"

"Horses," Con supplied.

"They got away – I hope. But father has something that one of them dropped."

Con scowled. His vestigial wings twitched. Jai noticed in passing that they had grown larger.

"Sis, the Kumatan are dangerous. We don't want them anywhere near our land."

"They were doing us no harm, just letting their beasts drink. They had children with them," Jai told him.

"I have never considered that Kumatan had children," Con admitted. "That notion almost makes them seem like us."

At that moment, both Con and Jai sensed the clashing of energies. Con tensed. They both waited, fearing the outcome.

"Hold my hand. We've got to alert the tribe," Con ordered.

Jai didn't argue. Stacion must have prisoners. That meant that the Kumatan would now come after him. She allowed herself to be dragged forward. On the second step, she fell into darkness and on the third she saw the village in front of her.

"What?" she asked in amazement.

"Later," Con spoke sharply. "Tell the women to pack and move to the hill camp. I must go and protect the sacred relics."

"Can't you just pack them and bring them?" Jai asked.

"No. Go."

Jai ran to the nearest group of elder women and gave the instructions. Within minutes, women were gathering their belongings from within the communal caves and ordering their children. Jai went to her own bed corner. She had little of value to pack, just her bedding and some tunics and modesty items.

Within an hour, the camp was deserted. Signs of the mass exodus were erased by the few warriors assigned to the camp. No one entering the village would think it had been recently occupied.

Con waited, hidden in the aura to protect the safety of the tribe's relics. He mentally dammed Lancho who was nowhere to be found.

Chapter 4

After everything was quiet, his half-brother lurched into the village and looked around in stupefied amazement. It was obvious that Lancho was drunk. Con felt nothing but scorn for him, but never the less, he didn't underestimate him. He removed all but the most basic of his protections from the relic cave before showing himself to his brother.

Even drunk, Lancho might notice if Con had erected shields more elaborate than the basic ones Stacion had taught him.

"Father is chasing Kumatan," Con said without greeting.

"Prisoners?" Lancho asked. His face became avid.

Con shrugged. "He usually gets some," he said, hiding his disgust. The tribe would be better off if Stacion didn't go out of his way to hunt their enemies. "I need your help. To put more shields here."

Lancho sobered up and looked at what Con had done. He snorted. "Pretty basic. Let me handle this. You go follow the others. Where did they go?"

"The hillside," Con told him, glad to walk away. He hoped that Lancho would act true to his usual form and take full credit for sending the tribe to safety and protecting the relics. He didn't want Stacion thinking he had that much initiative. Glancing back, he saw Lancho strutting like the sorcerer he would never be.

Con slipped away but not to go to the hill camp. His sister would see all was well there.

Instead, he went to try and see what Stacion had done this time. He couldn't limit Stacion's atrocities yet, but he could estimate the degree that the Kumatan would retaliate. Con had plenty of experience to judge by. The tribe had had to move at least once a year since he had become an apprentice sorcerer. Every time that Stacion had left his tribal lands to hunt the pale skins they had retaliated with force. When Stacion had captured some of them, the Kumatan came in to rescue them.

Con sighed. If only his father would leave the pale skins alone. It seemed to him that if the Atapi stayed on their own land and left the Kumatan alone, the Kumatan left the Atapi alone. It was a sort of 'if they don't see us, they won't hunt us' idea. It wouldn't happen. Stacion seemed to revel in rousing the wrath of the pale humanoids.

Con cursed aloud. "One day I'll kill him. If I don't there won't be a tribe left."

To do that though, he would have to learn about combat magic. And that would be the last thing that Stacion would teach him because the apprentice might challenge the master. And the apprentice might win – as Stacion had won over Mastro Ansuni – his sire.

Con had learnt a lot by watching Stacion without him being aware of it. But it wasn't enough. Sometimes, things that Jai knew filled the gaps in his knowledge. Not always though. Even so, Con knew things that his sire hadn't taught him. Things that Stacion possibly didn't know because they were, supposedly, women's magic. Con knew that the women's magic was not some insignificant chimera to make women feel powerful – it was real and it came from the same source as his own power. It was simply power used in a very different way and in his mind in a much simpler and more pure way. Ways that Stacion didn't know!

In fact, if Con was honest, he would admit that his sister's power was stronger than his own. She hid it well, and he was sure that the elder wise women conspired to help hide the fact. No one ever suggested it and Jai herself would not let him voice the idea. It didn't matter. A woman could not become a sorcerer.

Con finished running to the river and following it to the lake where Jai had seen the Kumatan. He waited, hidden in the aura.

After a time, four warriors, bearing two unconscious prisoners tied to long poles came into view. Neither looked any older than he was. Con stifled a hiss of disgust and continued to wait as the warriors passed him, oblivious to his presence. His sire had become predictable. He would lure the Kumatan after him, until they were on his land where his power was strongest. Then he would attack them.

Sure enough, more warriors appeared, as if fleeing. Close behind, the Kumatan guards ran with grim determination. Stacion was not with them and he must have done something to the animals or the Kumatan would not be on foot.

The pursuers slowed after crossing the river as if sensitive to the fact that they had entered the tribe's land. The leader urged them on but none of these pale skins had the power-feel of a Traeger.

There was a Traeger around somewhere and he must have attacked Stacion before he could return across the river. Con could feel the clashing of energies. The Traeger must have seen the pattern in Stacion's past attacks and been ready. Well, his arrogant sire would have to change tactics, Con thought. He was certain though that Stacion would move the fight back to his territory and the aura was being disturbed close by. He would wait and watch what the Traeger did and how Stacion countered it. He would see what spells and rituals Stacion used to attack and how the other reacted.

The disturbance in the aura was coming even closer. He sensed the ordered controlled magic of the Traeger. On that cue, he saw Stacion appear across the lake, leading the Traeger into a trap. The water in the lake quivered, two walls of force pushed the water aside and Stacion raced across. The pounding hooves of the Traeger's horse close behind. Six more mounted Kumatan followed the Traeger. All were within the lake when Stacion released the walls of force. The horses panicked when the water suddenly sought its natural position.

The Traeger, a fierce looking pale skin with hawk-like features quelled the panic with a wave of his hand and let his horse swim to shore. He urged it on as soon as its hooves reached dry land.

Con let both Stacion and his mounted pursuers pass before racing after them. They overtook the Kumatan that were on foot. No matter how fit they were the pale-skins were never able to match the pace of Atapi warriors.

In the deserted village, Stacion stopped running and whirled to face the horseman. Without pausing, he flicked his hand and a blade flew from it, swirling so fast as to be almost invisible. The horse screamed and fell as its two front legs were half severed. The Traeger rolled free and sprang to his feet, quickly erecting a magical shield that reflected the next blade back to the thrower.

Stacion hissed, slowed the blade and caught it. His next attack caught the Traeger from behind where he had not shielded. The whirlwind sucked the Traeger into itself.

Con edged forward for a better view. He had seen this used on a disgraced warrior. The result had been shredded flesh and globs of gore flung over a wide area. None of that was happening. He risked reaching out to the mind of the Traeger. There was no terror, no fear, just calm purpose. He stood in the very heart of the wind, somehow drawing power away from the deadly wall around him.

"I told you to go to the tribe," Lancho hissed and Con jumped.

"They're safe," Con knew.

"Why did you come back?"

"Same as you. To watch. To learn. He's the best, isn't he?" Con sneaked a glance at Lancho's face. He caught a fleeting look of some emotion before the smug 'you're just a child' look settled there.

"Better than you'll ever be - especially if he sees you here."

That was true enough, Con knew, but his half-brother had better be careful too. Stacion didn't like to share his fun. It was a good enough moment to slip away. Lancho would be riveted to the battle and waiting there to see the Traeger torn to pieces. He would also be anticipating the torture of the two prisoners. Now would be a good time to look at those prisoners.

Con slipped away, keeping a screen of trees between him and the groups of fighters. There were Atapi warriors guarding Stacion's cave and his relic store cave. Others were fighting Kumatan guards who were trying to reach Stacion's cave. As he slipped closer, he crossed a trail of blood - purple Atapi blood, not red Kumatan blood. It was clear that one of his tribe had crawled away from the village.

Con paused. He dare not interfere with the prisoners, even if he was disgusted with his sire for capturing children. They were still the enemy. And the Kumatan wouldn't stop trying to recover them. And Stacion wanted it that way. He would not tolerate interference.

As an apprentice devil, his duty was to help protect his tribe. He'd prefer to free the brats and get the Kumatan to leave the tribe alone. That being impossible, he tracked the trail of blood. He must help his injured tribesman.

The end of the trail led not to a wounded warrior, but to a young female who was curled around herself, stifling howls and rocking backwards and forwards.

He had not expected a female. They should all have gone to the hill camp – well before the Kumatan had arrived.

He squatted in front of her and asked, "Who did this?"

The girl stopped moving, her eyes widened in terror. Con spun around, expecting danger behind him but no one was there. Was she scared of him?

"I'll take you to the healers," Con told her.

"Don't touch me," she hissed. "Vile spawn of a thousand devils."

"You can't stay here. There are Kumatan here – very angry Kumatan."

"I want to die! At least they will kill me cleanly."

Con stared at her. She met his gaze and didn't look away. Facts fell into place. He glanced back along the blood trail to confirm his deduction.

"Lancho," he spoke aloud, to himself, not to the girl. She spat at him.

She might want to die, but she hadn't shown herself to the Atapi and Kumatan fighting with knives and swords that were getting closer and closer to the magic warded cave containing the prisoners.

He chanted a ritual and formed a bubble of silence around them both.

"If you wish to die – why don't you use your knife?" Con asked. An idea was forming. He might yet be able to help the prisoners if this girl would dare death.

"It is spelled not to hurt me. He made it blunt," the girl hissed.

Changing the topic, Con told her, "You should talk to my sister."

"The freak-born?"

"She has some minor healing skill, I am told." Con spoke carefully not betraying his knowledge of the truth.

"Why should I bother? I would rather die now."

"She was Lancho's first choice today." Con kept his tone neutral, careful to say nothing that might sound like condemnation of his brother or sire.

"I saw her walk out of his cave," the girl hissed.

"Did you see who entered before she left?" Con asked.

The girl nodded. In her mind was the picture of Stacion entering, Lancho leaving, then Jai leaving.

"Jai can help you," Con repeated his suggestion. He hoped she would consider it. The girl had power. Too much to waste in a senseless suicide.

"But he never even sees her," the girl said. "She is nothing to him."

"Perhaps," Con seemed to agree. The girl seemed to be thinking possible reasons.

"How did you leave Lancho's cave?" Con asked suddenly.

"I walked out. Crawled out!" The girl's eyes flashed with hatred.

Con knew that she didn't realise what she had done. Lancho wouldn't have finished with her. He would have warded his cave to prevent her leaving.

An idea grew in Con's mind.

"You devils are evil," the girl spat at him. "Will you be delighting in torturing children too?"

Con dared not answer with the truth. "I obey my master."

The girl looked as if she loathed him.

"Did you see Lancho with the prisoners?" Con asked.

The girl nodded. "He put them in the little cave and did some sort of pacing in front of it."

Con decided to plant an idea in the girl's mind.

"I want the Kumatan away from here."

"They won't leave until they have the prisoners and all their dead. You should know that."

Con eased a relieved breath. "Atapi are dying too."

The girl nodded agreement.

Con went on, "I," he stressed the pronoun, "Do not wish any harm to you. Nor will I let you risk yourself, unwilling."

The girl's eyes widened. Was she beginning to realise what he wanted?

"I think you were able to leave Lancho's cave because you and he had been – intimate. His magic was on you, so his wards didn't stop you."

She was about to hiss and spit again – but she swallowed the moisture and stared at the cave beyond. She nodded slowly. "I might die. Can you sharpen my knife?"

Con touched it and incanted a spell to negate Lancho's.

"I will distract the Kumatan," Con said. "When I do, run for the hillside camp."

The girl's eyes flicked to the prisoner's cave.

Con concentrated for a while and mentally located the energies of his sire and the Traeger, the Atapi warriors and the Kumatan fighters. There were several other non-Atapi energies. These covert ones were Kumatan – probably skilled assassins. These would be looking for the prisoners while the others were keeping the Atapi occupied.

Con slipped away, having worked out a route from shadow to tree to shadow, to avoid the covert watchers. As he left, he whispered, "Larcia protect you."

He meant it to tell the girl that he wished her well, and he was surprised when he felt the aura of Korvu beginning to swirl around her.

Now, Con told himself, it was time to end this obscene blood-magic feast. Enough was enough.

Con risked walking across planes to reach the trees near the lake. With all the energies being warped and woven, the slight perturbation of crossing planes from the village would not be noticed.

Once there, Con gathered energy and imitated the hunting horn the Kumatan used to communicate with each other. His own voice was soft, but its magic echo nearly deafened him. The three bursts travelled towards the village. He hoped the Kumatan would think the prisoners were freed.

Within moments, the energies swirling in the village changed. Con ran back. The girl was no longer in the cover she had found. He absorbed the energy of his sphere of silence. The Kumatan fighters were withdrawing. The Atapi warriors were racing after them, lusting for blood, believing their enemy to be running away.

None were looking at the prison cave so only he saw the two figures racing away to the trees where those other Kumatan energies were. None saw the Atapi female limping slowly away.

Con went to her, the quick way, crossing planes to go the short distance. He didn't want to be seen just then. "Come with me, quickly."

Con took her hand and ignored her hissed, "Let me go!"

"If you come now, no one will realise that those whelps escaped with any help."

"I don't care. I want to die."

"Let your hurts heal, girl. If you were worth nothing, would Larcia have protected you?"

"Are you a coward? Running away?" the girl challenged him.

Con ignored the insult. "I'm not suicidal," he muttered.

Suddenly the girl returned his grasp. "I'm Bernea."

Chapter 5

Con trotted back to the village the long way – step by step – not across planes again. He was pleased that Bernea had immediately sought out Jai. He sensed that something significant passed between the women, but the details were denied to him. The women had closed ranks around Bernea and tacitly frozen him out. He didn't let it anger him; he had simply stared at them and then turned to leave. He hoped that it meant that certain things would not be talked about. He recalled the group of women who had surrounded Bernea. Of them all, only Jai had acknowledged him. Siluci Danka had not been there. No doubt, that since he had succeeded in getting her with egg, she was avoiding him and the all-knowing old women.

Back at the deserted village Stacion's anger turned on Con as soon as the sorcerer spotted his youngest apprentice and he spread his huge wings and hop-flew the distance between them.

"Where were you? Why weren't you protecting the village?" Stacion hissed. The scent about him of blood magic almost made Con gag.

Con mentally translated the questions as, "The prisoners escaped and Lancho is blaming you."

"Master," Con chose the formal title, because right then he didn't want to remember who had sired him. "I was doing what little I was skilled at. I put what shields I knew on the sacred relics. I needed Lancho's help, since my skill is still basic."

Lancho, standing nearby, swelled with importance.

"He sent me to check on the tribe. I have been to the hillside and back several times. I came back here because I resented the desecration of our land by the Kumatan. I wanted to distract them so our warriors could kill them."

Stacion slowed his angry pacing. "Yes, they were dying." His face turned ecstatic as if he could still taste the death magic. He said nothing of the ten injured Atapi warriors, some now dead, some still lying untended on the ground.

"Where were you when the prisoners escaped?" Lancho demanded, grabbing him.

Con shrugged. "Not here, obviously. You had that cave so heavily warded that I had no need to go near there."

"The wards are still there," Stacion stated. "No lesser Kumatan or Atapi should have passed them."

"Perhaps the prisoners were the Traeger's whelps," Con suggested. "Maybe that male had enough power to free himself."

"Did you sense it?" Stacion demanded.

Con shook his head. "Should I have?"

"Maybe when you are older," Stacion allowed, dismissing that idea. "You should have helped kill our enemies – did you even sense their scouts?"

Con feigned ignorance. "I wasn't here that long each time. But, Father, I'm no warrior. If I tried to use a sword…"

Lancho's laugh came exactly as Con anticipated.

"You'd cut your own head off," he roared. "You little coward."

It suited Con to let his father and brother think he had no fighting skills. So he drew himself up, and pretended his dignity was smirched.

"I was protecting the tribe! I was doing my duty as a devil in training. One of the women was left behind. She was injured…"

"The women all left," Lancho shouted. "If they didn't, it's your fault…"

Con shrugged, not admitting that he knew about the girl and Lancho.

"She left a blood trail that a blind Kumatan infant could follow. I took her to the hill camp."

Lancho suddenly realised who the woman might have been and he seemed itching to go and check.

Con nudged his brother's mind with a lie. "She was babbling prayers to Larcia - would have killed herself if she had had a weapon."

"But I had her warded! How could she get free?" Lancho blurted.

"I thought the Kumatan had got at her. I saved her so that she could breed warriors for the tribe."

Con saw his sire's face turning a dark shade of purple. Energy began leaking from Stacion's aura. Con thought through the ritual for a breeze and imagined the energy reaching to the dying warriors that Stacion had not yet given permission to be tended.

"I had – in my power – two bargaining pieces," Stacion snarled, his anger pulsing towards his sons. "You!" he roared at Con, "You useless creature. Go tend the warriors. Don't show your face until the elder warrior tells me you know how to kill with a blade."

Con knew this was a dismissal and escaped with relief. He went quickly to where he sensed the injured warriors, and subtly gathered the energy sloughing from his father to return to these men. He could still hear his father roaring at Lancho, but his father had slipped into an ancient dialect used only by sorcerers. Of course, Stacion did not realise that Con knew it. Surely didn't know that the elder women knew it. They had taught Jai, who had then taught him. Con smothered the thought. If the women had secrets from the tribe's devil, something was seriously amiss. One day, Con would look into those secrets.

For now, his mind relished Stacion's tirade to Lancho. Of course, his half-brother had taken full credit for sending the tribe away, shielding the sacred relics, protecting Stacion's cave and the prisoners. Apparently he had so belittled Con's efforts, that now he had to take credit for the failures.

"Master Con," the Elder Warrior approached him. "We are awaiting orders."

"Tend the wounded," Con said quickly. "Prepare the dead for the death rites. Put the dead Kumatan in the cave near my Sire's. No doubt he will instruct you on how he wishes them prepared for being returned to their palace."

The Elder Warrior barked orders, and then he spoke softly to Con. "So, Master Con, you are useless as a warrior and I must teach you?"

Con nodded, allowing a slight smile to touch his face. It was quickly gone. It was not needed to be said that Con was actually more skilled with a sword than most of the young warriors his age.

"Right then, young master. Tomorrow, at dawn."

Con nodded. Later he would suggest that in the time scrounged from his duties, when he had been practicing his fighting skills – he could learn unarmed fighting.

"What can I do to help the injured," Con asked.

"Can we take them to the healers?" the Elder Warrior asked.

Con listened to the continuing tirade and considered his Sire's mood.

"Send for the healers to come here," he decided. In Stacion's current mood, of blaming everyone but himself, he would probably claim that the warriors were deserting if he allowed the injured to be moved.

As if in agreement, he felt the aura of Korvu stirring. A power was drawing off more blood energy from his sire. It was draining into the injured.

Con sat near the injured warriors, watching the other warriors pack cloth into bleeding wounds and bind them in place. They offered the injured water and bathed their sweating faces. His attention was drawn back to the shouting match between Stacion and Lancho.

"The whelp was right about one thing." Stacion was saying. "The women are needed to breed warriors. Our numbers are declining."

"But you said…"

Stacion slapped Lancho and the sound echoed around the village. "I did not give you permission to play with the woman. Had she been found by the Kumatan, the rest of the tribe would have been in danger."

"But I had her warded!" Lancho argued.

Another slap.

"She crawled out through your flawed wards. No doubt the prisoners did the same. Did you try your tricks on them first? Did you deny me the right to them?"

"There's no way…"

"You used magic on the woman – didn't you? Magic to make her give you what no woman would willingly give! With your magic all over her – no wonder your wards failed. They thought she was you!"

The listening Con hid a smile. Stacion wasn't finished. "You've been learning magic for fifty years and you still don't know that? What did you do to my prisoners?"

"Nothing! I swear," Lancho yelled. "It had to be Con, or the girl."

"Shut up, fool! That male whelp was a Traeger's brat. Do you know what I could use him for?"

"Controlling the Kumatan?" Lancho suggested desperately. He knew his father expected an answer.

"That and more. I could warp his mind to spy for us. He would tell us everything about our enemies. I could make him a tool to poison our enemies' minds…"

Stacion fell silent, ignoring Lancho's desperate babble of, "It had to be Con."

"Silence, fool. The woman is up the hill. Con took her as he said. They arrived before the horn blew for the Kumatan to run off like cowards."

Con was startled. The women had lied. To support him? No, they would be protecting the girl and him only incidentally. Another instance of unstated knowledge.

Finally, Stacion's voice reduced from a roar. Con could still hear his words as echoes in his mind.

"Very well, we will test your claim. You go and repair the wards on the cave – exactly as you had them before. We will see if Con can get through them."

With that much warning, Con took a bowl of water and a cloth from a warrior and began to wash the face of the nearest injured warrior.

The summons, when it came was not presented as a roar. Stacion walked to where Con crouched and picked him up by his neck. The effort was minimal. Stacion was almost a foot taller that Con and extremely strong. Con's weight would be nothing to his father.

Con hung limply and remained silent. He sensed that his sire was going to use him to humiliate his elder apprentice. It would be better to pretend that he wouldn't enjoy it. Stacion walked with Con still in his grasp, over to where Lancho was muttering words for the magic wards.

"So – will my warriors live?" Stacion asked as he dropped Con to his feet.

"Five are dead. The other five will recover." Con hoped that was true. "They killed fifteen Kumatan. I ordered healers to come to them."

Somehow, Con knew that only the 'killed fifteen Kumatan' really registered on his sire. Stacion merely nodded. He was watching Lancho.

"You – little apprentice – will attempt to break through the wardings on the cave. If you can it means you might have done it already. Of course, if you did, I would be very angry. Now, so that you will try your hardest, I will tell you my incentives. If you get through them, I will teach you the magic of the wind blades – after having you thrashed. If you can't I will simply have you thrashed – for stupidity."

Con dared not ask what the rules were for his half-brother. From the way Stacion stared at Lancho, he was sure his sire believed he had been lied to.

Lanch wiped sweat from his brow. Was he hoping Con could break his wards – or not? As he continued pacing and muttering, Con considered his position. He really, really wanted to know how to make and control the wind blades. Craved it. Yet he didn't want to succeed and give Lancho a way out of his plight. He hadn't passed the original wards. And from the way Lancho was acting, maybe he had indeed tried to interfere with the prisoners.

Con also knew he was really not in a position to win. He would be getting a beating either way, and even should he win he doubted that Stacion would immediately teach him the magic he craved. He might have to wait years.

The other problem was that to break those wards – he would have to use magic that Stacion had not taught him. Yet he would have to look like he was really trying.

Chapter 6

Con collapsed into a limp heap just inside the cave Stacion used for some of his rituals. It was the one that contained the dead Kumatan, the one that Lancho had warded and from which the prisoners had escaped.

He hurt. Every inch of his skin was grazed; every nerve was sending pain messages to his brain. Still, it could have been worse. Stacion had used his own version of beating – one that didn't involve him getting his hands tired using a stick. He had called up his devil wind and had it buffet him inside.

If Con had not sensed how that Traeger had protected himself – he would have lost all his skin.

This was his punishment for 'stupidity', for having only been learning magic for ten years, not fifty like Lancho or three hundred years like his sire.

Lancho crawled into the cave and went a bit further before he collapsed. Con opened one eye and saw that his half-brother looked worse than he did himself with large areas seeping blood and his wings, the physical evidence of his sorcerer ability, looked battered and broken.

Con wondered about his own wings. They hadn't grown all that much yet – certainly not enough for him to fly.

It seemed that if the label 'stupid' applied to any of them, it fit Lancho better. After fifty years as an apprentice sorcerer, he should have learnt ways to protect himself from his sire's rages. Had he ever learnt anything that Stacion hadn't taught him? Knowledge doled out in miserly dollops by a sorcerer so loathe to share his power.

Con stretched out his arm so that his fingertips just emerged from the cave entrance. He had drawn on the aura of Korvu during his slow crawl from where the whirlwind had dropped him to the cave. He had started to heal, as his sister had taught him, but in that cave, his awareness of the aura was blocked. As that small trickle of the natural aura came to him, he felt the contrast of that to the atmosphere in the cave which was warped and vile.

Lancho, however, seemed to recover quickly. He seemed to drink in that vile energy like it was water. He was up on his feet; his skin scabbed over, when Stacion strode in exuding his own sensation of satiated satisfaction.

Con felt Stacion's glance pass over him, heard Lancho's mutter of 'weakling' and was relieved to be dismissed as temporarily useless. He wasn't actually as helpless as he pretended, and he wasn't deaf either.

"The Traeger's scavengers are skulking across the river – waiting for us to discard the husks of their dead invaders." Stacion paced the cave as he spoke.

"Have you a use for the trash?" Lancho asked in a tone full of respect for his master.

"Perhaps collecting their rubbish will prove a useful distraction." Stacion spoke slowly.

"While you do what?" Lancho asked in the still respectful tone.

Con wondered the same thing, but he doubted that he could have managed the same toady attitude as his half-brother.

Stacion reached into his belt pouch and drew out something that glittered in a shaft of light from the entrance. Con moved imperceptibly so that he could see the object.

"This belongs to one of them," Stacion said, studying the item. "Probably the female. It is the sort of thing Kumatan females like. I think that whilst they worry about their trash – they won't be guarding the whelp."

"Traeger's don't usually collect the trash. Isn't it below the dignity of a slave master to do a slave's job?" Lancho asked.

"I think I can make it his job," Stacion snarled a grin. "That one wasn't so skilled. If the cowards hadn't been recalled – there would have been one less Traeger."

Con didn't believe Stacion's boast, but he hoped that whatever Stacion planned, that he would have no part in it. In fact, he was telling Jai that as he tried to predict what Stacion was contemplating.

"He thinks he can draw the girl back here," Con added to Jai. "He thinks the shiny thing is hers. And he still has the dead Kumatan here."

Con had to stop thinking at his sister when Stacion stalked over to him. Once again, Stacion lifted him as if he were a baby animal. His scrutiny was unnerving.

"You're not as weak as you are acting," Stacion remarked before sending a surge of energy into Con who jerked until he controlled it.

The energy made Con feel as if insects were crawling all over him and biting him everywhere. Unlike the calm energy of the aura of Korvu, this made Con feel twitchy and angry.

Stacion studied him a while longer. "Good! It seems I didn't whelp a coward or weakling. I suggest that while you learn to be a fighter that you practice healing yourself. Or you will be dead within a week. I will insist that the Elder Warrior is not gentle with you."

"Why should he be, Master? No enemy would be."

Stacion bared his teeth in his version of a smile. Con was dropped to his feet.

Stacion turned from him and said, "We have work to do and little time to do it. Sharpen your knives. We begin at once."

Con obeyed, darting glances at his sire as he honed his knife. The shiny object was on the small rock altar, out of reach. Stacion was not considering it just then. His gaze was directed at the dead Kumatan. He didn't explain what he was going to do – he just began and expected his apprentices to watch, learn and copy.

It didn't take long for Con to be glad that the tenuous link with his sister had broken when his finger had been pulled into the warped aura of the cave.

Stacion was carefully dismembering a Kumatan body, starting with the ears, then the eyes, then the nose. After that he severed the head, both arms and both legs. Then he separated the legs and arms at the knees and ankles. Exactly fifteen pieces, if you counted the torso.

With difficulty, Con began duplicating the actions on a second body. It took all his will to overcome nausea, to harden his mind to obey. He dared show no more weakness or Stacion would snuff him like a candle. He needed to become hard if he was to one day fight his sire. He would need to be hard if he ever became the devil of his own tribe. He must be hard enough to do anything necessary to protect his tribe – even killing.

All that helped was the idea that the bodies were just empty husks but the intended result was obscene.

There was a tacit tradition that after the ritual for their own dead, the Atapi would return the dead Kumatan to their brethren. The pale skins gave great respect to their dead and respected the Atapi devils that returned the bodies so funeral rites could be held. Certainly, it appeased them. This time, Stacion had not yet performed the ritual for his dead warriors. He was making the Kumatan wait. And while they waited, he was creating an insult to the Kumatan dead.

Con thought that Stacion certainly knew that the Kumatan would be angry. That he was giving them even more cause to hate him and to want to destroy him and his tribe. Was he so arrogant to think that he could prevail against the massed might of all the Traegers?

Con considered how this insult would be received and had to agree that in light of the dismembered bodies – one safe at home child would not enter their minds.

When the fifteen bodies were in fifteen pieces, Stacion proved that he was not finished. Using his magic, he took one piece from each body and fused them into a grotesque new whole. Lancho copied this new magic with lustful glee. Con fought the desire to flee into the fresh air. With determination – he forced himself to copy his sire's efforts. He tried to seem to be concentrating on the magic – not a rebellious stomach.

Sending the bodies back in pieces had been bad enough, but at least the parts could be ritualised together. Stacion's magic had made the gesture of returning the husks an obscene gesture. The joins were vivid and the effect was crude…

"Con! Fetch the Elder Warrior."

The order needed no second bidding. Con raced for the entrance. He sent the Elder Warrior into the cavern and took the time to be sick. Then he gestured for more warriors to be waiting outside the cave and for others to bring shrouds and stretchers. He felt his sister nearby, trying to reach his mind. He blocked her. He was not ready to share this 'lesson' with her. She would probably know from that briefest of contacts that he had been doing something vile.

Con returned to the cave and waited by the entrance. The Elder Warrior had his orders and was leaving. His face was unreadable. He saw his warriors waiting outside with the things he needed and he gave Con an approving glance and continued without stopping.

His instructions to his warriors were succinct. In moments, fifteen warriors, carrying shrouds and ropes entered the cave. Each wrapped and bound a reassembled husk and carried it out to a prepared litter.

None of the warriors spoke, but Con used an ability that was believed to be an ability restricted to the tribe's devil. He tested the minds of the warriors and learnt that the procession of bodies was to be slow – one by one – to keep the Kumatan waiting as long as possible.

"They know their job, little brother," Lancho said, distracting Con from sensing what the warriors thought of the mangled husks. "You are to rake the floor about the altar."

Con dragged his mind back to reality. He moved to obey, not surprised to be made to do such a menial task. Stacion did not encourage people to enter his working cave.

The rake was within and Con began working in silence. He had no trouble hearing Lancho giving orders to the Elder Warrior for all warriors not involved in the removal of the rubbish to patrol the boundaries of the village to keep everyone out. Stacion prowled the deeper areas of the cave where many of his power relics stood in dark alcoves.

Whilst Con continued to rake away the signs of the butchery into a pile outside the cave entrance, Lancho was sent to retrieve items from amongst the sacred relics. Con watched his half-brother without being obvious. Stacion must have given him a talisman that would enable him to pass the new wards that Stacion had placed on them. Yes, Lancho was swinging something around. It looked like the paw of a wild canine. Those creatures, the same kind as would scavenge the muck he had raked out – had better not come too soon.

Con re-entered the cave to go over his previous raking, wondering now, why the sorcerer wanted the blood removed when he normally didn't care. It certainly wasn't a good time to try reading his father's mind. It was always a risk when he tried it with his sister or others that Stacion might read his mind while he was doing it.

Fortunately, he had learnt that Lancho had no such skill. Stacion had boasted that only a sorcerer of great ability and bonded to his tribe could do it. Con knew otherwise. He knew that the healers could do it. Women. And he, Con, a mere beginning apprentice could do it. It made him more open minded about magic. Lancho thought the heavy handed rituals of Stacion Ansuni were the only way to use magic. Con was young enough, keen enough and frustrated enough to learn from anyone. He would learn from the wild canines if they had magic. His strength would be in his unexpected methods.

Lancho returned as Con raked the last of the debris from the cave. He left the raking tool just inside the entrance and followed Lancho with an appearance of subservience.

Stacion had donned rich robes that covered his folded wings. This told Con that serious magic was to be performed as the robes were one of Stacion's most treasured power relics. Usually, Stacion preferred to display his huge wings – which were big enough for him to fly with and bigger than those of most of the other tribal devils.

In spite of his apprehension, Con was excited. This opportunity to watch his sire doing major magic was a rare event. He felt his sire reading his mind and sensing his excitement. Let him think that Con was keen to be part of the spell to summon an innocent for torture.

Chapter 7

"This fell from the arm of that Kumatan female," Stacion stated, lifting the shiny circle of crystals from the altar. "That female was here. This object links her to here. It can be used to bring her here."

Con considered the logic. He knew Stacion could find someone by touching something belonging to that person. He could walk across planes to a person bearing one of his tokens. This was similar, but different.

Con felt his mind and Lancho's being caught by Stacion. Then he saw darkness, like the darkness between planes. Then he saw somewhere else – a vision like he had never imagined. He automatically memorised every detail of the strange place even though he had not the words to describe it.

He tried to - a square cave with dangling fabric at each side of a square view of the outside. A long square object was raised off the ground with a rich fabric draped over it. In the middle of that drapery was a creature like he had never seen before. It was curled into a ball. As his mind observed it, it woke and arched its back. Con could almost hear it hissing.

"It's a pet! See, it's got something around its neck," Lancho observed.

Con hadn't heard of 'pets' but he noted the collar which seemed to be plaited from multi coloured threads.

The creature stalked across the surface it had slept on and jumped daintily from it to another square object. This one had a square of some strange substance standing behind it. The creature walked in front of the substance and a second creature appeared.

"It's a mirror," Lancho told Con, aware of his ignorance in the mind link. "The Kumatan like to stare at themselves."

The creature began to make a loud mewing noise. After a while, a Kumatan girl entered through a moving rectangular panel.

"Yes!" Stacion hissed and he began to chant.

Con controlled his thoughts and began to chant along with his sire and half-brother. Stacion placed the shiny object on the ground, and the three of them began circling, forming a vortex of power above the shiny object. In his mind he still saw the girl, now cradling the strange beast in her arms. Its fur was standing straight out. The girl looked frightened and was trying to move the rectangular panel. He sensed Stacion holding it shut and was awed by the sorcerer's ability to affect things that were so far away.

Stacion began to circle faster, and a vortex of power was now forming in the place with the girl. Her long hair was whipping about her face and light objects were being flung about the room.

Con wondered if noise was audible outside the room and if help would come to the girl. It seemed that Stacion caught the thought for with a twist of his mind the girl and her creature vanished from the room. His mind now saw her in a dark place. It was the darkness between planes and Con knew then what his father was doing.

The creature looked frantic; it was writhing, trying to get free from the girl.

The warriors had quickly moved aside when the healers arrived. The women, even the two old ones, must have run at full speed to arrive so quickly but they were no more out of breath than the returning warrior messenger.

The Elder Warrior told the uninjured warriors to stand guard around the entrance to the cave where some kind of sorcery was being performed.

Jai went to work immediately, as did the two older women. The injured warriors were in a bad way – left too long before being tended. She controlled a surge of anger at her unacknowledged sire. These warriors had lost a lot of blood before having the pads pressed on their wounds.

When Con had called her, he had said he was drawing power from their sire. He hadn't said it was tainted with the blood of the dead. Yet in a weird way, it made sense. The power from the dead, who no longer needed it, was keeping these honourable warriors alive and would not be available to a dishonourable sorcerer.

"Con?" She tried thinking at her brother. She had no contact with him since he had called and told her what she was needed for. The women had been ready when the messenger had arrived.

"Jai?" Con's tone was full of pain.

"What is wrong?" Jai thought back as she drew power from the aura to help the injured.

"I'll live," Con assured her. "Lancho claimed that I broke his wards so the prisoners could escape. Stacion set a test. I was to try to break Lancho's wards."

"You didn't!"

"No, but I had to look like I was trying," Con told her.

Jai had a fleeting summary of the whole test. Her brother seemed to be trying rituals that he hadn't been taught; things he might have seen done but not fully understood. Very subtle.

"But you are hurt!" Jai protested.

"My punishment for being young and stupid," Con grimaced mentally. "Lancho is worse. At least I had figured how the Traeger survived in Father's whirlwind. He, I think, believes Lancho interfered with the prisoners."

"So he was punished for bring incurably stupid," Jai commented. "What are you doing now?"

"Trying to seem weak and useless so Father doesn't involve me in what he plans next. He thinks he can draw that Kumatan female here. He has some object of hers."

Jai felt the mental contact vanish. She glanced in the direction of the cave where Stacion worked his magic.

When Bernea came close to her, to check the bandages on the next warrior, Jai whispered to her.

"Stacion will try to bring that Kumatan girl back using some bauble of hers."

Bernea shivered. Her own ordeal was too vividly fresh in her mind, though now she no longer wanted to die, she wanted revenge. "Can we do anything?" she asked very softly.

"No." Jai shook her head. "We cannot interfere."

"Your brother?"

"He must obey his master."

One of the old women moved closer. She had heard the quiet exchange.

"Magic is limited by the understanding of the wielder," she said as if telling them a lesson.

"I understand that it isn't wise to provoke one's enemies," Jai said.

"That girl isn't my enemy. She trusted me," Bernea stated.

The old woman moved away again, saying only, "Maybe it isn't wise for the two of you to be seen here. Neither of you are beloved of sorcerers."

"Maybe we should bring Siluci here," Bernea suggested slyly.

The woman made a rude noise as she moved further away. Jai was thoughtful.

"What's up?" Bernea asked, sensing it.

"She's right," Jai announced.

"What?"

"She means we shouldn't be seen by those who have already been thwarted once today," Jai said obliquely. "And I pray to Larcia, that however he intends to get that girl – it won't work."

She saw the understanding in her new friend's eyes.

"Keep close to me," Jai said. "I have learnt how – to not be seen."

The warriors had noticeably improved. Their wounds had closed, and they were sitting up even though they were still weak from loss of blood.

Bernea nudged Jai and shoulder shrugged in the direction of Stacion's cave. "There's Con."

Both watched as he approached the Elder Warrior and gave no sign of seeing them.

Jai reached out for his mind, and felt him close her out. She shivered. His aura had felt – dirty. When she saw him being sick, she knew he had been doing something vile. Bernea was about to make a comment but Jai shook her head.

"Some things are best left unthought, unsaid. Tacit secrets," Jai told her friend, as she continued to infuse energy into the warriors and urging them to drink the herbal infusions the old woman was brewing over a tiny fire. Bernea continued to watch Con, seeing him raking out the cave.

After a while, Jai felt a lessening of the power she was drawing on to heal with and hide herself.

The older women were aware of it too and their glances went towards the cave but they said nothing. The few remaining uninjured warriors looked uneasy.

"I think you should join in patrolling the edge of the village," Jai quietly suggested to the nearest warrior. He was the most senior since the Elder Warrior had gone to answer Con's summons. Many of the warriors had gone into the cave and brought out what had to be the Kumatan dead. "These warriors no longer need you and soon they will be well enough to guard the entrance to the cave."

The warrior gave no sign that he had heard Jai speak. He would have ignored her except that his warrior senses were agreeing with her. After a moment, he snapped out orders to the others who obeyed him at once.

The once injured warriors pushed themselves to their feet and took up their weapons. The two old women began to gather their things, slowly. They gave no indication that their two younger helpers were still around.

Bernea was watching the cave, half hoping to see Con Ansuni. Jai was slowly shifting herself around, sensing the power vortex and knowing what was being attempted. When the strain on the aura suddenly ceased, she looked around more frequently.

"What was that?' Bernea pointed.

Jai caught sight of a fleet footed grey creature, streaking towards the trees. She turned and saw her brother racing after it. Then she sensed a nearby presence and gripped Bernea and dragged her to a mound on the ground.

"That's her! The prisoner," Bernea said. They both glanced around. All the warriors were staring after the strange creature.

"Lancho," Bernea warned, even as Jai was re-establishing the hiding field of the aura.

"Stay still," Jai warned. "Very still."

Lancho moved steadily forward, seeming to be tracking the creature, though it had not come anywhere near them. He passed close to the three women without seeing them. The Kumatan girl roused from her dazed state and saw him. She tried to struggle away. Jai and Bernea moved quickly to hold her still and cover her mouth. Bernea met the girl's frightened stare and put a finger to her lips. The girl's eyes widened as she recognised her previous rescuer. Bernea brushed Jai's hand from the girl's mouth.

Sensing the girl's terrified reaction to the sight of Lancho, Jai knew that he must have tried something with her. The girl relaxed when Lancho moved away.

Bernea had turned back to watch the cave, and she saw Stacion Ansuni emerge. She gasped as he spread his wings and flew. Jai watched dispassionately.

"We can't stay here," she said. "But we dare not move."

Bernea shrugged a shoulder in the direction of the sorcerer and Jai nodded.

They were both relieved when he flew out towards the trees, but a moment later, Jai pushed the girl down and flung herself over the stranger. Bernea copied the act.

The two old women, their packs full, sprinted to near where the young women were, then slowed to a walk. They looked up, saw the sorcerer and bowed low.

The sorcerer forced his mind on theirs and saw the vision of Jai healing and demanded aloud, "Where is she?"

"Majestic One, she returned to the village when we had no further need for her."

"When?" The women imaged a period of time, when they hadn't seen Jai.

The sorcerer flew off towards the new location of the village.

Jai sent a burst of emotion at her brother. Con walked into sight within moments.

"The village – now!" Jai urged.

Con kept his gaze away from her companions.

"Touch me," he ordered. Jai understood, and pushed the other two into contact with her brother.

"Walk forward," Con snapped.

The hillside appeared around them. Jai raced off. Con didn't look at the other two, just said, "Walk again."

Bernea realised that they had appeared in a tiny cave that overlooked the gathering area. She released Con, and grabbed the stranger's arm. Con moved again and vanished. The Kumatan girl clung to Bernea, her eyes wide with fear.

"We'll be alright," Bernea said just loud enough for the Kumatan girl to hear. "We just have to stay in here."

The Kumatan girl eased her grip and Bernea looked at her.

"Why – are – you – helping – me?"

Bernea was amazed to hear the girl speaking Atapi even if it was with a terrible accent.

"I…" Bernea began, and then she stopped. Her reasons were complex. At first she had wanted to die. Wanted the prisoners to kill her or the Kumatan warriors to kill her. Now, Jai had given her a reason to live. And now she knew that Jai had secrets. In the end she shrugged and said, "Jai wanted to help you."

"Jai? Your – name?"

Bernea was startled. "No, I'm Bernea."

"I – Suzi Mosellan."

A dark shadow crossed the entrance of the cave. Suzi shrunk further back. Bernea put a fist in her own mouth. Then she removed it to mutter, "Larcia guard us."

When the shadow of Stacion Ansuni had gone, Bernea crept forward. The sorcerer flew and hovered then flew to a different place overlooking the narrow valley and hovered again.

"He – is – looking – for – me," Suzi's voice was trembling. "He – wants – to do – horrible – things – to me."

Bernea didn't comment. She shivered too, remembering what Lancho had done to her and what he had promised to do. This strange Kumatan girl was no older than she was herself. But Bernea could not bring herself to think of her as an enemy. So she crept to the back of the cave and squatted beside the stranger to give her what comfort she could.

Jai crept into the cave, well after dark, bringing food and water. Bernea embraced her fervently.

"I have been so scared."

"You have been brave. Both of you," Jai assured Bernea.

Suzi crept forward. "You – Jai?"

Jai was startled. "You speak Atapi?"

"Yes – some. I am Suzi."

"You must be hungry," Jai suggested, putting off what she was going to say.

"Yes," Bernea admitted and Suzi nodded.

"I have been hearing a lot of noise," Bernea said. "What is happening out there?"

Jai glanced out of the cave. "The women have prepared a celebration."

Suzi made a sound of protest. "Because – you – killed – so – many – Kumatan?"

"Atapi died too. More barely survived," Jai said quietly, understanding her disgust. The women were using a celebration to assuage Stacion's rage.

"I'm – sorry," Suzi apologised, and she meant it. "I – don't – mean you – personally."

Jai touched the girl's arm. "I know. Not all Atapi are warriors."

"I – don't – know – why – you – helped me, an enemy," Suzi said, turning to where Jai's silhouette was vaguely visible in the entrance.

"All Atapi are not like Stacion Ansuni," Jai told her. "And I am not helping an enemy."

"Oh!" Suzi exclaimed quietly, confused.

Jai changed the subject. "The women are celebrating life," she explained.

Suzi said nothing. Bernea muttered, "You're alive!"

"Yes," Suzi agreed, still uncertain what Jai had meant earlier. "Why – did – you – bring – me here?"

"It is an Atapi place, protected by Atapi warriors. We are safe here," Jai told her.

Suzi laughed nervously. They seemed to imply that no one would look for her here, but she tried to imagine hiding an Atapi in her father's house.

"How – long – must – I – stay?"

Jai shrugged. "Tell me how you got here."

Haltingly, sometimes groping for words to explain when she didn't know the words she needed, Suzi managed to tell her story.

It fitted with what little Con had told her.

"Some power picked me up and dragged me into blackness. All the time Crystal was trying to jump from my arms. I daren't let her go or she would have been lost there. At first I thought I was about to faint, but then I realised that it was like darkness through which father took Jenha and me home after we escaped. Like how you got me here. Then I began seeing the place we escaped from, and Crystal got free and I fell."

"What's a Crystal?" Bernea asked.

"My cat. A pet. Can you find her?"

"I saw it race from the cave – it was fast," Bernea commented.

"She isn't used to being in the wild. She won't know what to do," Suzi moaned.

"Suzi, I'm sorry, but we can't look for it," Jai told her.

Suzi drew in a breath. "I understand. It is only an animal."

"No! I wish I could, but Lancho and Con are hunting it."

Suzi gasped in horror.

"I would have thought Lancho would prefer to be drinking fermented hare's milk at the feast," Bernea commented.

"And Stacion would never forego a feast in his honour," Jai agreed. "But Lancho and Con would be wise to appear diligent just now."

Suzi wondered if her knowledge of Atapi was failing her. Oh, she understood the meaning of their words, she thought, but they seemed to be saying something else.

"Has your cat, the pet, ever run off scared before?" Jai asked. "I don't know what they do."

"Father's hunting dogs chased it once. It climbed a tree." Suzi grinned at the memory.

"Huh! No animals we hunt climb trees!" Bernea commented.

"Crystal comes from off world," Suzi explained. "I want to get more and breed them. They catch small rodents."

Jai wondered what 'off-world' meant, but keep the word in her mind for later. In her mind, she suggested to Con to look in the trees for the animal. After a moment, she heard in her mind, "Got the little beast. Has the heart of a warrior, the teeth of a canine and wriggles like a snake."

Jai spoke. "Con has her."

"What," Bernea asked.

"The cat. Con has it."

"What will he do?" Suzi asked.

The answer came with an angry mewling and a deeper shadow in the cave entrance. The source of the noise smelt like snake. Jai wrinkled her nose.

Bernea took the animal from Con, holding her breath as she took it back to Suzi at the back of the cave.

The Kumatan girl made cooing noises at the cat and the noise became a purr. She didn't seem to notice the smell.

Con stayed at the front of the cave. "Sorry about the smell. I remembered that snakes have a strong contaminating magic so I shoved the creature in a snake hole."

"Do you mean, he summoned the creature?" Jai asked, amazed. Con merely remained silent and Jai knew that she had guessed right.

"I'll take her back," Con said softly.

"No, I'll do it," Jai argued.

"You have never crossed planes by yourself," Con said. "You should be able to, but…"

"I can do it," Jai insisted. "You've got to be careful."

"I am. I won't be going near the feast. He might be getting drunk by now, but he won't forget today too soon. I'll settle for him leaving angry Kumatan alone for a while."

Suzi approached and said, "Thank you."

Con reacted to her voice but did not answer her. "I had better go back to hunting that creature."

He turned and left.

Suzi wondered why he would go on hunting something that he had found, and then realised that he had tacitly said he hadn't seen her. "Why did he shove Crystal in a hole?"

Jai realised that Suzi's use of Atapi had become more fluent. "Stacion had a shiny thing. He thought it was yours."

Jai waited for Suzi to figure it out.

"Crystal's collar? I dropped it near the river when we had to flee."

"Your creature has good instincts," Jai told her. "If you had kept hold of her he would have got you."

"But…"

"The snake aura is strong enough to break the link between the collar and the creature," Jai explained.

"Smell is strong enough too," Bernea added.

Jai suddenly turned away from the others and hissed, "Quiet!"

She sensed Stacion's mind seeking hers. She squatted and imaged herself doing a natural function; pictured the disposal place as it appeared in moonlight. She felt the flick of a command to come to him and his rapid withdrawal.

"I have to go to him," Jai told Bernea, who understood. "You should go and show yourself amongst the women. Leave after me."

To their guest, Jai said, "Stay in here, and keep your creature with you. You will be safe here. Larcia will protect you."

Jai slipped out, avoiding warrior sentries and returning to the gathering area from the direction of the waste pit.

Bernea waited a while longer. She really didn't wish to face anyone — but Jai was right.

"Don't be afraid," Bernea told Suzi.

"I want to go home," Suzi said.

"Of course — but — trust Jai, please?"

"Why are you both risking yourself for an enemy?"

"I can't think of you as an enemy," Bernea admitted. "Not now."

"Before?"

"When I first saw you, I was hurt, angry and wanted to die. I hoped you would kill me."

"Now?"

Now, Bernea couldn't really explain her feelings. "Some things are best not thought about, not talked about. Tacit secrets."

Suzi didn't understand, but she nodded.

Chapter 8

"You?" Suzi said doubtfully.

Jai stood proudly. "I can do it."

"But…"

"But you want to go home," Jai reminded her. She ignored the sense of Suzi thinking, "You're only a girl."

"Con?" Suzi suggested.

"No. It wouldn't be wise."

"I'll stay longer?"

"It won't be safe to stay much longer," Jai understated the truth.

"What are you afraid of?" Suzi asked noticing that Jai was agitated. "Don't talk in riddles."

"I want you back where you belong," Jai said.

"Do you no longer like me?"

"No, I mean, it's not that. If you go back now – then maybe your people won't come and try to wipe out the tribe for what Stacion has done."

"Taking me?"

"That and worse," Jai whispered.

"What? Tell me!"

"No. Don't ask me," Jai begged. "I can't talk of it. I'm not supposed to know. I have to take you back, now. They won't miss me for a while."

Suzi sensed the urgency. "Ok, I'm ready." She made a clucking sound and the cat jumped into her arms.

Jai took Suzi by the arm and said, "Think of somewhere, where you live, where we can arrive unseen."

The vision Jai shred was so strange that she didn't feel comfortable reaching for it. Yet she had to hurry. Con had told her that Suzi had power like the Traegers – but untrained. Jai trusted that and decided that if Suzi held onto the vision, they could do this together.

"We have to walk three steps," Jai said, pulling Suzi gently.

"That's what father did. I remember."

Holding hands – one brown with the feel of fine scales, the other pink flesh – they moved together, neither thinking the other dangerous.

Jai felt the initial wrench, saw the blackness and the strange place at the end of it. She felt Suzi's relief to be going there and her own excitement at seeing how the Kumatan lived.

The room became real around her, Jai turned and stared. It wasn't a fever dream. Her relief at successfully crossing planes was short lived. A loud clanging noise erupted and she had to clap her hands over her ears.

Suzi went at once to the door and locked it. "It's the intruder alarm. I've locked the door. You had better go."

Jai couldn't concentrate on a picture of anywhere. The noise hurt her ears. Then it stopped, someone was banging on the door. She thought of the cave in the hill camp and began to walk, but something like a wall blocked her.

"Father, NO!" Suzi suddenly yelled.

Jai turned and saw the tall Kumatan male in the room with a weapon aimed at her and something changed inside her.

"What the...," Suzi began. She was astounded. Where Jai had stood, was a pink skinned girl. She could have been Kumatan, but with bigger eyes.

The Kumatan male took a step back. He stared at the intruder as he demanded, "What is the meaning of this Suzelaine? You disappear for two days and now there is an Atapi creature in your room?"

He began to walk towards Jai, who backed away.

"Father! You are scaring her. She saved me – helped me." Suzi put herself between her father and Jai.

"She's Atapi!" Suzi's father said fiercely. His expression betrayed his anger. "She? You can't even be sure it is female. Only males can change their shape. Is it here to spy? To take you again?"

"No," Jai said, daring to stare at him. In this form she understood his words. "To bring her back."

Suzi butted in. "I didn't run away, father, I was taken away. Some vortex of energy – caught me and Crystal. Your shields didn't stop it. It entered the room as easily as you just did. It dragged me into darkness, like when you brought Jenha and me back. Crystal freaked, and got away from me as I began seeing the place where we were prisoners. I fell onto the ground outside. If Jai and Bernea hadn't protected me, I'd be getting tortured now."

"Do you expect me to believe that? That Atapi women would disobey the tribe's sorcerers and give aid to an enemy? Do you expect me to believe that a female – no older than you can do what only sorcerers can do?"

"Sorcerers and Traegers," Suzi dared to point out.

"A Sorcerer who would murder my children would not worry about placing a spy in my house as a target for his magic. That's a more likely scenario. He would use her to bring his warriors through your bedroom to kill us all."

"What has made you so angry, Father? Because you didn't know I was in danger? I can understand that. But Jai didn't take me – she brought me back – by herself."

Her father didn't answer. He just glared at Jai. "Does he know what you are doing?"

Jai knew who he meant. "No," she admitted softly.

"And if he finds out? What will he do?"

Jai didn't answer. Some things were best not thought of. The Traeger made an effort to control his anger and hatred since she was not acting like a cornered Atapi.

"Why would you protect an enemy?"

"There are no bad things between us," Jai said, looking at the Kumatan male.

"You saw no threat in a young Kumatan female?" the Kumatan suggested.

"I…She didn't belong in our tribe's place. I brought her back – for the safety of the tribe."

"How could one, barely adolescent female, be a threat to Stacion Ansuni's tribe? And how could one, barely adolescent Atapi female do something that Stacion Ansuni couldn't do better."

"Keep me alive, Father," Suzi stated.

"Very well, how could one very young Atapi female snatch you from the clutches of a sorcerer as powerful as Stacion Ansuni? That I would like to know."

"Father he was using…"

"I was asking your…guest," Suzi's father silenced her.

"I was told that magic is limited by the understanding of the wielder," Jai said carefully. She saw a thoughtful expression cross the Kumatan's pale pointed face.

"That village was deserted. Only your sorcerer and his warriors were there. Why were you there? Had everyone returned?"

Jai sensed a purpose behind the question and was wary. "Healers were sent for – to heal the injured warriors. The old women told me to come. I have a small ability and could help them."

"A healer," the Kumatan nodded as if that explained something.

"What were you trying to heal here," he snapped.

Jai stayed silent.

"You know what he did! Don't you?" the Kumatan accused. "Was he bragging about it?"

"He does not discuss his business with females," Jai said.

"But you knew about it. You brought my daughter back now – to appease me. So I wouldn't send squads of guards to destroy your village – your tribe."

Jai's eyes went wide with horror.

"Father! All Atapi are not like Stacion Ansuni. Jai is not."

"After all things that evil monster has done to our kind – nobody cares. I have permission from the Kimh to destroy him and his. His warriors are as bad as he is and the women are only there to breed more monstrosities."

"Con wasn't like that – tell him Jai." Suzi urged.

When Jai didn't answer, she went on, "He took us away from the deserted village and found Crystal for me. He didn't betray my presence."

"Con? Con Ansuni I presume - if he can cross planes. He is Stacion Ansuni's youngest whelp. If he knows about you – I have no doubt his sire does too."

Suzi trembled and walked to the bed to sit down. She looked at Jai, now with distrust in her eyes.

"Is it true?"

Jai nodded, very slightly. "Con is his son, but he is not like him."

"A very commendable sense of loyalty to your lover," the Kumatan said with sarcasm. "He is young – but no match for Stacion Ansuni. In time he will be as bad – or dead. Stacion has so far outlived over twenty of his own sorcerous whelps."

Jai wished herself taller and the strange body she wore seemed to grow upward to be of equal height with the taller Traeger.

"I have no quarrel with you if you seek out Stacion Ansuni and even Lancho and pit your might against them. There is bad blood between you and them. But if you succeed in destroying the whole tribe, then you Kumatan and whoever the Kimh are will be no better than he is. No – you'd be worse. Killing a whole tribe – men, women and children just because more Kumatan died that day than Atapi died. Well, I call upon Larcia, Protector of Atapi, to shield my tribe, to protect those worthy of her help and to deliver those who endanger the tribe to justice."

"Atapi justice? I don't think so," the Kumatan spoke with sarcasm again, but he glanced around the room because as a Traeger he could feel power stirring since the girl had spoken.

"You can't threaten me," he growled at Jai, who had shrunk back to her first size. "I know that Larcia is a myth for superstitious women. I'll let you go – to tell your lover that his days are numbered as are those of his sire and the other apprentices."

"Con is not my lover," Jai said, moving further away from the Kumatan.

"Brother," Suzi suggested, surprisingly perceptive.

The Kumatan made a grab at Jai, but she dodged him. "You are also his whelp! You must be – you have too much power."

"No. No male owns to me. I'm nobody. Useful as a healer, that's all. If I truly had magic – I'd have died at birth."

Jai wanted to flee. The odd walls seemed to close in on her. The Traeger – he had to be one – was divining her secrets. She could feel his anger and loathing. She pictured the village, forgetting in her panic that it was deserted. She ran towards the Traeger, who tensed for an attack. On the second step, she fell into darkness, unable to complete the third step.

She sensed him nearby. Heard him speak to her mind. "Foolish child! I have a shield on my house to warn if your kind tried to come through. I activated another when you intruded."

Jai imaged herself curling into a small ball, for she could feel nothing, not even herself. Terror froze all thoughts in her mind. She didn't move, even when the presence finally went away.

Chapter 9

Jellarn Mosellan returned after fruitlessly searching the deserted Atapi village for a trace of the female. He should have been able to sense her anywhere nearby. He'd felt her mind – he had hoped to use her to find where her tribe had gone. He was certain that she would hurry back to warn them.

He returned to his daughter's room and sought there for a trace of the Atapi girl. Reluctantly, he recognized her bravery – for facing him. Or was it ignorance? He sensed nothing. How had she escaped from his shields? They were set so that he was the only one who could pass them.

"A female – with power that strong," he mused aloud. He had never heard of such a thing – well except for that Atapi myth about Larcia – the she-devil. Was that girl unique?

No, she had said that if she truly had magic – she would have died at birth. Did Stacion, and the other devils, kill females with strong magic at birth? Why? It made no sense. That girl had strong magic. Stacion should have been able to sense it as well as he, Traeger Mosellan could.

He didn't like mysteries.

Another mystery. Why had she brought Suzi back after Stacion had taken her again? To sneak in on his blind side? Was Stacion using her to get to him? No that didn't make sense either. Stacion would not waste energy taking his daughter again just to send her back – not after that unspeakable act he'd performed with the dead guards. Could the girl be working against her sire? If she really was Stacion's whelp?

Jellarn shook his head to clear his musings. He needed more information. What did he know?

Stacion had captured his children. They had escaped with the help of an Atapi female. Illogical, unlikely, but his children didn't lie to him. So if it wasn't some kind of illusion – did Stacion know that one of his women had freed his prisoners? No – or the woman would be dead and Stacion might not have taken revenge for the loss of his prisoners by dismembering the Kumatan dead. He had ensured that attention was not on his rescued children when he tried to reclaim one of them. His daughter, innocent, harmless, less able to defend herself and Stacion could try again.

His children must move to safer quarters. He would see to it quite soon, he must do several other things first. His shields must have been faulty. His mind released the energy that held the shields and he created them again from nothing. Now, as soon as an Atapi intruded, the intruder would be frozen in place.

He needed information. Jellarn strode along the passage to the far end of his large house where he had a shielded room. He had a prisoner there. An Atapi that had once been one of Stacion Ansuni's warriors. The warrior had been broken; he no longer tried to escape. He had become a useful source of information.

"Obaki?" Jellarn strode into the room without giving warning.

"Yes, Master?"

"Stacion Ansuni's female whelp – what is her name?"

"Master, he has none. He only whelps males."

"I have heard of one. Who is she?"

"Master, unless she was born since I came here, I know of none. Is there a female which you think is his?"

"What do you know of the one called Jai?"

"Jai? Oh yes. The freak-born. I know of her. No male admits to whelping her. She is not Stacion's. He would know his own blood. She was training to be a healer, and therefore was useful. Though without an acknowledged sire, no warrior would wish to mate with her."

"Would she be likely to do things without Stacion's knowledge?"

"No master, No woman would – they are obedient and he can touch the mind of any – whenever he wishes. He would know if they were disobedient."

"Really?" Jellarn feigned disbelief. "And your mind?"

"Master, I have not felt him in my mind since you brought me here. I think that he thinks I am dead."

An idea occurred to Jellarn.

"If he knew you were here, alive, would he act to rescue you?"

"Master, I was a warrior. If I could not defend myself and rescue myself I am of no use to the tribe. Should I return, I would die."

Jellarn stalked from Obaki's prison. His anger with Stacion Ansuni flared anew. When his guards fell into Atapi hands, he fought with all he had to get them back. He would have gone back for the dead, except the Atapi usually returned the bodies after their own rituals for the dead. Too bad he couldn't use Obaki to lure Stacion to him.

He should have asked what Obaki meant by "freak-born". That could wait; he had to make sure his children were safe.

Jenha and Suzi were talking in Jenha's room when Jellarn walked in without knocking.

"Father!" Jenha stood quickly when he saw his father.

"I want both of you packed to move in half an hour," he stated.

"What?" Jenha queried.

"Why?" Suzi asked.

"If Stacion Ansuni is making his hatred of Kumatan personal – I will not have my children at risk again. You will stay in the palace."

"But he wasn't after me!" Suzi argued.

"I will not have you at further risk. Get packed."

"Father, listen. I think the sorcerer made a mistake," Jenha said. "I think he was after one of us, but it was Suzi's cat that was the focus of the spell."

Jellarn listened and considered. "Explain."

"Suzi told me that he had the cat's fancy diamond collar. He must have thought it was Suzi's. Remember, she dropped it by the river?"

"So how do you come to that conclusion?"

"Jai told me – when I asked why Con had shoved Crystal in a snake hole. He must have told her," Suzi explained.

"A snake-hole?" Jellarn queried.

"Yes – it was something about the snake aura being strong enough to break the link between Crystal and the collar."

Jellarn almost smiled. Snake aura – he had heard something about that long ago, but dismissed it as meaningless trivia. But apparently not useless. And proof that Con and Jai did not want Stacion to have Kumatan prisoners.

Suddenly the sense of his son's comment came to him. Stacion had made a mistake. And it was as Jai had said about magic being limited by the knowledge of the wielder.

"Tell me everything – from the beginning," Jellarn suggested, settling himself in the one chair in Jenha's room. "Everything you saw, felt, heard and thought."

Jellarn listened intently, asking questions to clarify points. At the end of Suzi's narrative he asked, "What do you think was meant by "some things are best not thought about or talked about?"

"I'm not sure, father," Suzi admitted. "I knew enough Atapi to understand what Jai and Bernea said, and I have told you all that and you probably accept it literally, but I couldn't help feeling they were referring to other things that they both knew but didn't want to talk about."

If Stacion could read minds at will – it might be fact. He considered all he had been told, without revealing his thoughts.

"Father," Suzi asked tentatively. She got his attention.

"Yes?"

"You aren't really going to destroy the whole tribe, are you?"

"It won't be my decision," Jellarn said quietly. "But you have given me much to think on. Like the idea that Stacion's tribe don't all follow him blindly. And that it is possible for Kumatan and Atapi to be friends."

"Jai is my friend. And Bernea too." Suzi stated.

"I cannot promise you that no harm will come to the tribe," Jellarn said truthfully, "Because I cannot let Stacion Ansuni continue his reign of terror. If it takes every Traeger on Korvu – we will render him harmless."

"Include that Lancho Jai mentioned," Suzi shuddered remembering what that one had wanted to do to her.

Jellarn nodded. "However, by destroying the tribes sorcerer - we may well destroy the tribe. They will have no protection from natural dangers, Atapi outcasts from other tribes, and sorcerers trying to enslave them. They would be leaderless."

"There's Con," Suzi suggested, hoping for hope.

Jenha dashed it. "He's no older than we are. He'd be no match yet for an old experienced sorcerer."

"If I thought he could defeat his sire, I'd consider supporting him. But I agree it isn't likely. Stacion has already outlived over twenty of his talented whelps."

"But if he had our help," Jenha suggested, "Maybe this Con could do it."

"Son, if he is like you, young, full of confidence, sure that his old man is senile – it wouldn't be enough. Stacion is ancient. It might be better for us to incite all the other devils against him."

"I like that idea," Jenha admitted.

"Enough," Jellarn ended the discussion. "Pack your things. I will be back in half an hour to take you to the palace."

He ignored the resentful looks of his children as he walked out.

Chapter 10

Jai felt that she must have been asleep for she became aware of darkness. Then she remembered where she was – and nearly panicked. The memory of Con's instructions for crossing planes came to her. He had talked of this situation, and had a solution. Think of a place, and image walking there.

The cave where they had hidden Suzi came to mind. She didn't want to be seen, so she pictured its entrance.

Imagining herself walking forward in the darkness, Jai felt the wrenching as she crossed planes, and was relieved when the force that had stopped her had gone. The heat of the sun on her back reassured her, but made her wonder how long she had been trapped in the darkness. Had she been gone long enough to raise unwanted questions?

She looked around to see if her arrival had been noticed, and was stunned to see, not the view of the hillside camp, but a vista of red, sunlit sand and scrubby grass tussocks.

She knew where she must be from Con's descriptions of the Rock of Arkor, but she had not tried to come here. She was a female – she was not allowed to be there. This was the most sacred of all places to the male sorcerers.

Her curiosity overcame all caution. She might never get another chance to be where she most dreamt of being. According to Con, the sorcerers could sense when someone came near the rock - and they did not tolerate intruders.

"You are not an intruder," a female voice spoke in her mind. Jai spun around but no one was visible.

She was at the entrance to a cave, so she ventured in. The cave was dark compared to the brightness outside, but her eyes were capable of adjusting to see in the faint reflected light. No one was within the cave.

"Who are you?" Jai asked aloud.

"Come, my daughter, have you forgotten? You invoked my name, my protection for your tribe and before that for the sake of a child of another race."

"Larcia?" Jai asked in awe. "How could you possibly still be alive?"

"I live in the aura of the rock," the voice said. "My body is here, needing neither food nor water. For long periods, it is as if I am asleep – until one who believes – invokes my name. First your brother, now you."

"Did you bring me here?" Jai asked. "Or did I do something wrong trying to cross planes?"

Jai heard faint mental chuckle.

"I interfered a little."

"Why?"

"It has been such a long time since I have sensed one with such power, so pure."

"I'm a freak," Jai told the voice. She had been told that often enough.

"You are a perfect creation," Larcia said. "Like one of my daughters. It has been so long since one has visited me."

"I have as much power as my brother, yet all I can do is what the women can teach me – about healing. Con shares what little Stacion teaches him – but I cannot be seen doing any of it. Women just don't. And a lot of what Con learns, he won't teach me."

It was a novel idea to Jai to have someone to talk to with whom she did not have to guard her tongue.

And she knew in her soul that this was no trick. She poured out all the indignities, all the frustrations, all the humiliations of her life. She revealed in that narration so much detail of the tribe's life that she sensed Larcia stirring to anger.

"I have been asleep for so long," Larcia admitted. "That is not how things should be."

"I would like to learn how it was," Jai admitted tentatively.

"And you shall," Larcia promised. "This place, where you are, will be your place to dream and to learn. What do you know of the other tribes?"

"Only that they exist," Jai admitted. "I think I know more of the Kumatan than of other Atapi tribes."

"Yes, your young pale skinned friend," Larcia agreed. "Even between the three great races of Korvu, the balance is broken. That friendship is a step in the right direction. The three races were once equal – each had its role and the aura protected all. Now it seems that only I remember and I am old, and cannot leave here."

"Teach me," Jai begged. "And I will teach my brother Con, so he can be like your sons were and not like our sire Stacion Ansuni."

"So ambitious, your sire. So powerful," Larcia recalled. "He was full of plans to regain the prestige of the Atapi. His lineage was impressive – from my oldest son in direct descent. When he did his dreaming, I called him Stak. He has changed..."

"Yes," Jai agreed. "It is not the Atapi that are important, nor the tribe – just that he gets what he wants."

"Your mother was proud to be chosen as his mate," Larcia recalled. "She invoked my name so that she may produce a child worthy of so great a sorcerer. She also wished for a daughter, and that her children would grow to be strong protectors of the Atapi. I did not hear from her again."

"Father had her killed. He claimed when she laid two eggs, that she had insulted him and mated with another male. Then when we hatched, he took Con for his and I was none of his and whoever claimed me was a traitor."

"Your sire had indeed grown arrogant. He never realised the great gift he was given and now – he will never know."

"Arrogant and greedy," Jai agreed. "He teaches Con in miserly dollops. Even Lancho is ignorant and he is four times Con's age. Con has to learn by watching him and sensing the energies and that does not teach him all he needs. It is only when Stacion wants to draw on Con's power that he becomes free with his teaching."

"I sense from what you are not saying that he has discovered the great energy liberated by death."

"Yes," was all Jai said.

"He must change," Larcia stated. "When you return to your tribe I will use you to focus my sight. My body cannot leave here but my mind can travel in the aura."

"Is there anything that you can do?" Jai asked.

"On my own, little. With help – maybe much. I remember your womb mate when he came as a young child. I felt his promise then. Tell him he is welcome here."

"And Lancho?" Jai asked with a sly wish to know what Larcia thought of him.

"Should that one come here again, he will not leave," Larcia stated. "And you, daughter, should return before your absence becomes an issue. Remember though, this place is yours to dream in and to learn in. No one else shall find it, unless you wish it. It is exactly like the cave on your hill camp. To get here imagine that place and think of me."

Jai was a realist enough to realise Larcia was right. She needed time to think about everything she had experienced in this hectic day. There was a lot to tell Con.

"Will you go?" Jai asked Con after relating her experiences in the privacy of his cave.

"Not yet," Con considered, squatting next to where Jai sat on one of the floor furs. "When I have learnt more. When things around here quieten down. When I am sure the tribe is safe from Kumatan retaliation. From what you said of that Traeger, Stacion has gone too far."

"You could challenge him," Jai suggested.

"I hardly know any fighting skills," Con reminded her. "And even though some of the healing magics have potential to reduce the effect of his magic, I haven't been able to practice them to see how I can best use them."

"I will be supporting you," Jai promised.

"I know you will be, but – not yet."

Jai didn't press her brother. She didn't relish the idea of open confrontation with Stacion either.

"Did anyone miss me?" Jai asked instead.

"Lancho wanted to know where you were. He sent me to ask the women. They explained to me that after the effort you put in to heal the warriors – when you foolishly expended yourself – you were probably sleeping still."

"Is Bernea alright?" Jai asked suddenly. "He hasn't been after her again, has he?"

"I don't think so," Con said thoughtfully. "Or if he has, the elder women scared him off. Perhaps that is why I had to ask about you."

"Should we tell him about the Kumatan threat?" Jai asked.

"You definitely should not!" Con said. "And he doesn't need a whelp like me telling him. He expects them to come, welcomes them. However, I will place wards of my own about the village to warn me if they come here. I will defend the tribe if he does not."

"Won't he sense them?"

"They are basic rituals," Con shrugged. "It will probably amuse him, like my warrior practice session this morning. He and Lancho watched – sharing their views of my efforts. I don't know about him, but I could easily take Lancho if he stooped to such non-sorcerer levels as to challenge me with only a sword."

"I wonder if Lancho will insist on trying again for his secret name?" Jai pondered aloud.

"Of course," Con insisted. "After all, he thinks he is the greatest sorcerer since Stacion Ansuni. Why?"

"Something I forgot to mention. Those secret names – they come from Larcia. She creates them from the sorcerer's lineage. She said though, that should Lancho came back, he wouldn't leave."

"I hope he will try, don't you?" Con asked.

"I'm not so sure," Jai countered. "I detest him, but right now he is a buffer between you and Stacion."

"You are right. Without him, I will be the target of all his attention. More than now."

"I could contrive some gossip," Jai suggested. "In such a way that no one will know I started it. Siluci would challenge Lancho with it. She thinks that she can order everyone around now she is Stacion's mate."

Con laughed faintly. "Go for it. He doesn't deserve our help but I would rather Stacion drain him to the dregs before me. I don't think Stacion will let him try again too soon. He would rather have two apprentices to augment his power."

"So what happens when you get your secret name?" Jai asked. "What's the big deal?"

"What I heard, is that when you are given it – the master apprentice bond is broken. It means that you can block your master from your mind and he can't use your power anymore. I don't know how."

"What if he later finds out your secret name?" Jai asked, thinking about something Larcia had said that she hadn't though important until now.

"The secret name is a thing of power. It helps you invoke the aura. No sorcerer would willingly tell his secret name – if another knew it, they would have power over that sorcerer."

"I know---," Jai said slowly. "---his."

Con stared at her. When she began to speak again, he silenced her with a finger on her lips. "Not now. Not a thought. Not a word." He evoked the tacit silence.

Jai nodded. She understood.

Con Ansuni went on, "Kumatan scouts are intruding on our territory. He knows they are there, but he is doing nothing. He calls them bird-witted fools. I think that they are deliberately keeping away and just looking like they want to find the new village site. Perhaps they hope to draw him away from his warriors so they can swat him."

"Or Larcia is protecting us," Jai averred. "Is there more to the threat?"

"It seems so," Con admitted. "Our esteemed sire is convinced that other tribal sorcerers are plotting against him. And that is a real threat, if the Kumatan are taking their anger out on all tribes."

Chapter 11

In her dreaming place, Jai asked the presence in her mind, "Could you make him forget about me?"

She was practicing a minor ritual to make some small coloured rocks tumble endlessly together in a rock bowl.

"Your sire?" the mind voice asked.

"Of course," Jai agreed. She pictured a tiny Stacion Ansuni being tumbled with the rocks.

"If he forgot who you were," the voice finally replied, "he would think you a stranger and try to kill you."

Jai sighed. Larcia was correct. In Stacion's current state of paranoia, with him convinced that the other sorcerers were out to get him, strangers died quickly. And if he tried and failed, he would realise she was protected. Then he would go all out to break Larcia's protections. And then he would see what Larcia had hidden from him – that her power was as strong as Con's.

"Well, what about making him unable to see me?" Jai tried. "Then I could sneak up behind him and put a blade in his back."

"He has himself too well protected," Larcia sighed. "I cannot interfere with them."

"Could I?" Jai asked.

"Not yet. You would have to understand each layer and learn to negate each one. You have much to learn before you do that. You will need to learn all that he knows and probe his understanding for weaknesses and strengths."

"How can I learn all he knows? He won't even teach Con all that," Jai said annoyed.

"If you can confuse his mind reading, you should be able to read his, if you are subtle," Larcia told her.

"Will you teach me?" Jai asked.

After a brief pause, "Yes."

"Why?" Jai felt the need to ask.

"Because you see that the Atapi must change back to the way they were," Larcia said quietly. "You knew that even without me trying to mould you. Your mother wanted her children to be protectors of the Atapi – she knew. She believed too."

"Do you think Stacion senses that?" Jai asked. "I know he can't sense my power, but since that Kumatan raid and his failures, he has been watching me. And warning off anyone who seems too friendly to me."

Larcia saw in her mind the nature of those "warnings". "You have true friends who won't be frightened off. Does he stop Con talking to you?"

"If we are seen together, he sends Con off," Jai admitted. "So when we meet, we both cross planes to a secluded cave. It is a risk. If he were to touch our minds and see us together, he would be angry."

"You can ward your mind at such times," Larcia told her. "I will tell you how. I think, though, that he fears you."

Jai stopped the rocks tumbling, being startled by that remark. "Me? What have I ever done to make him fear me?"

"I did not say he had a reason," Larcia said quickly. "As you believe, he knows who sired you. He stole your mother from under the nose of the "Old One", that's the most powerful sorcerer from all the tribes. Stacion kept your mother well-guarded for months before he coupled with her to ensure she had not already been got with egg. Your mother had magic potential – was certain to breed sorcerers."

"I'm surprised that he killed her then," Jai said, her old anger rising.

"Are you? When you say he prefers not to share his power?"

"But he can draw power from his whelps that have magic," Jai countered.

"Too many - he would find distracting," Larcia seemed to be implying something Jai couldn't figure out.

"It is rare for women to lay two eggs," Larcia told Jai. "But it is not unknown. My own mother did."

Jai thought about that. "So even though he denies you ever existed, he fears that I might be like you?"

"It is possible. The lore learnt at his mother's breast is not easily forgotten."

"So, because he knows I can heal, he is afraid that I will suddenly get vast power?"

"And I think that he senses your resentment, over and above that which he is causing throughout the tribe."

Jai began her magic again. The rocks resumed their tumbling. Eventually the rocks would be polished smooth.

"You can tie that ritual to the aura and it will continue without you being here." Larcia told Jai how to do it.

Jai recalled her image of Stacion tumbling with the rocks. Too bad she couldn't tie him to the image and make it real. Eventually, she promised herself, Stacion Ansuni would die – preferably by her hand.

"He's getting paranoid," Jai commented.

"It is no more than he deserves," Larcia told her. "In times past, if a sorcerer endangered his tribe – he would be challenged. If he endangered all tribes, other sorcerers would challenge him."

"But if one of those others won, my tribe would be no more than slaves to his," Jai pointed out.

"That would depend on whether the successful challenger had a tribe of his own already. Or your brother could petition the Old One for help. He is in fact your mother's sire. And he is still more powerful than Stak."

"Forgive me if I don't trust such family ties," Jai said. "Con told me what Stacion said about the Old One. Ask him for help and we would be in debt to him, forever. There has to be a way where I can help Con."

"That would be the best way," Larcia agreed. "Tradition demands that the sorcerer must win by himself. Do you have any ideas?"

"Yes, in that case, don't get caught helping. Other than that, no. If I had a blade that would negate all his power, I still would have no chance of getting near enough to him to use it. Con doesn't feel ready yet."

"An answer will come," Larcia counselled. "All knowledge of all sorcerers is recorded here on the rock."

"Even his?" Jai asked.

Larcia was silent for a time. "Some, but he has added nothing for a very long time."

"Either he's learnt nothing new, or nothing he wants to share," Jai murmured.

"No matter, you can still learn from him. Meanwhile, read the writings of Socon, my eldest son."

Jai left her rocks tumbling and retreated to a ledge to one side of the cave's entrance. Here on the flat rock, runes became visible. They seemed to be etched into the rock, but glowing enough to be visible. Jai settled down to decipher them.

Since her earliest visits, reading had become a delight for her. Larcia had taught her what each symbol meant and given her access to the magically stored information. Until now, she had been reading Larcia's words and now reading her son's words she noticed the difference. The symbols were drawn in a slightly different way and the tone of the writing was like hearing a man speak, not a woman.

The first writings were obviously done when he was young, newly made a sorcerer. He seemed to be proud of his achievement. And when describing the ritual for his new magic he also wrote of how he had come to discover it.

The attitude of the writing was on going and Jai found that comparing his writing with Larcia's overview of the same ritual was enlightening. It made her mind open to possibilities. It suggested to her that if she couldn't find a ritual to do what she wanted, she could create one. Snippets of rituals seemed suggestive of what she wanted – if only she could copy them to think on later.

"Bring a piece of clean hide and some charcoal," Larcia suggested. "I'll teach you to write."

Jai kept thinking on bits of ritual, trying to piece them into the shape she wanted. She tried to do this only at the cave in the rock, not that in the village. Her problem was that she wasn't exactly sure of what she was trying to do. She was considering that problem at the village cave when Bernea crept in.

"Jai, Siluci is due to drop her egg soon. She demands you come," Bernea blurted.

With an effort, Jai pushed her musing aside. She had warning of that fact, although she had not acted on it. It would be very unwise to admit knowing - particularly as she had learnt of it from Stacion's mind – when he had thought her asleep. Stacion had been far from willing to have her assist with the laying of his next whelp.

Bernea helped Jai to her feet.

"I suppose I had better go to her then," Jai said without enthusiasm. She risked a passive touch on Stacion's mind. He wasn't with Siluci – the Elder Mothers had sent him away.

She really needed to teach Con the trick of doing that. Knowing what Stacion was up to could be useful for him as would be blocking his mind from Stacion reading his. Con hadn't wanted to know Stacion's secret name yet, but if he knew it now, he would have it when he might need it. He wouldn't have to use it. It was a useful bit of sorcery for her to have figured out.

Jai used the ability to block Stacion when she wanted to do things or think things without the risk of him "seeing" or "hearing" them. At those times, she would put a ward on her mind by thinking of her sire's face and using his secret name to tell him what she wanted him to see her doing. If not sleeping, then doing some useful task like weeding the herb garden, along with thoughts appropriate to the task. So now she removed the warding on her mind that showed her mind sleeping. If Stacion checked now, he would see she was going to help his mate.

She had learnt that by keeping his face and secret name in her mind, she could passively sense his thoughts and actions. As she had sensed that he had left his mate to her labour, she had also sensed a lack of concern for Siluci. What he was considering was the best way to use the whelp, if it was male.

Jai hadn't tried to sense too much. His mind was often full of exquisite ways to torture his perceived enemies. Though his contemptuous thoughts about Lancho amused her, and his belief that Con was still ignorant enough to be no threat to him relieved her.

Jai trotted rather than ran to where the Elder Mothers had Siluci.

"What kept you, freak born," Siluci demanded as a contraction rippled across her swollen abdomen.

Jai stared at the younger woman, then without a word, turned and walked away. Siluci screamed at her to come back.

"Perhaps, daughter, some respect," an old woman suggested to the gravid younger. "If you cannot respect the person, you will not respect her skill and she cannot help you."

"Jai! Help me please," Siluci screamed.

It was the closest to acceptance that she was going to get, so Jai returned without comment.

"Will you work with me," Jai asked Siluci.

"Yes, yes. They say you are the best," Siluci begged. "My mate agrees."

Jai knew better, but said nothing. She hoped that Stacion would not blame her if anything went wrong.

The atmosphere in the birthing cavern was full of scented smoke, to help relax the patient. Jai began to speak softly to Siluci, telling her what she needed to do. This was her first egg and she was tense with fear because of the pain.

Using the aura, Jai helped Siluci to relax as she examined her and felt the egg within her. Siluci was small and slender. The egg was large.

The elder healers added more herbs to the brazier and began a low chant. Jai began to massage the opening where Siluci's egg was beginning to show. The shell was firm, but flexible, as it should be.

Soon after, she helped Siluci into a squatting position over a pile of soft animal hides. Jai talked gently and encouragingly to the younger girl, and when she sensed the pain increasing, drew on the aura to ease it. The laying would be painful for the girl's muscles were stretched to splitting point around the egg.

At last, after several hours, the egg dropped. The elder women eased the chanting and gathered around Siluci to congratulate her. Jai used the distraction of their chat to repair the tears and splits that Siluci had suffered. One of the women took the egg to keep warm near a thermal vent.

After the fragrant smoke had cleared and Siluci became more clear headed, the women began instructing Siluci on her duties to the egg for the two weeks until it hatched.

"Surely Jai could do it?" she said. "Better than me?"

Privately Jai agreed, but instead she said, "If I were to do that, the whelp would come to think me its mother."

It was enough to change Siluci's mind. She listened to the elder women with more concentration.

Jai finished cleaning up and slipped away.

"Siluci dropped her egg," Jai told Con as she served him his evening meal. "The eggling is strong within."

"Could you tell what it will be?"

"Not for sure, but probably male."

"That will please Him," Con commented. "Has he looked in on it?"

Jai shrugged. "I expect he will when it hatches and he can judge if it will be a sorcerer."

Their eyes met in an unthought moment of total understanding.

"I will hear how it progresses," Jai said obliquely. She knew Con would care.

Con nodded and changed the subject. "Lancho's gone."

"Gone – dead?" Jai asked hopefully.

"No. Stacion has sent him somewhere," Con told her. "I don't know where, just that I have to take over Lancho's duties as well as mine and keep close by Him."

"Let me teach you how to block him," Jai suggested yet again. When she saw him about to disagree she went on quickly. "Better now before he judges how much power he can drag from you. So you can block his efforts."

"Won't he be suspicious if I start to block him?"

"He hasn't noticed me doing it. I had better show you now as we probably won't be able to meet so often in future."

Con agreed. "Teach me."

"You already have the basics," Jai began. "You are able to touch other minds with yours."

"The sorcerer's over-mind," Con agreed. "But I can't rely on it – except with you."

"It is because you have the ability, but it isn't directed. A lot of the old women have it like that. But you need it before you can sense another mind trying to touch yours."

"He is never subtle," Con commented.

Jai rolled her eyes at him. "When you sense that, think on the word that I tell you, picture the face and think of what you want him to see or hear. He won't sense it – it's a passive magic."

"You've tried it?" Con saw Jai smile.

"Then, to sense his thoughts, picture his face, think the word and imagine he is talking his thoughts aloud."

"What about others, will it work on them?"

Jai shrugged, "You would need a different word."

Con thought for a moment before realising what Jai meant.

"And I think," Jai went on, "that you need to have an image you can use when he wants to drain you of energy. Something like a deep well with a false floor half way down. He can reach that point and think he has it all."

"Have you tried it?" Con asked.

"No, he doesn't think I have enough to be more than mildly useful as a healer."

"What's the word?"

Jai put her mouth to Con's ear and breathed Stacion's secret name.

A feral smile was Con's only response. "And he won't be able to use mine, for I haven't one yet. Yes, yes, I know. He doesn't need to while I am his apprentice."

"But – when you are ready for yours, go alone," Jai told him.

"That's not how it is done," Con objected. "The master sponsors the apprentice."

"That's how it is done now. Once it was not. You are welcome there any time, Larcia said. And I think that if he went with you, he would learn your name."

"I will remember," Con promised. "It is nearly dusk, he wants me then…"

"Be careful," Jai whispered as he slipped out into the fading light.

Chapter 12

In the cave in the Rock of Arkor, Jai found the peace that was now lacking in the village of her tribe.

Her latest distraction was Siluci calling for her every time she imagined something was wrong with her egg. Jai hoped that when the whelp hatched she would go to the elder mothers for advice.

It was bad enough that there seemed to be an increasing number of intrusions into the tribe's territory. The village was often stripped of all but the injured or old warriors. At those times, the women would send their whelps into the caves and be armed with their hunting knives ready to defend the village.

Many of the abandoned village sites had been visited. The signs that were left angered Stacion. He could be heard threatening vengeance to the perpetrators, but each time those responsible were long gone.

He believed that the junior sorcerers from every other Atapi tribe were responsible, and couldn't seem to decide where to start retaliating.

Con had managed to tell Jai that he was busy playing "rabbit" to the Kumatan "hawk"- and keeping that enemy out of the way. He had thanked her for her lesson about hiding his power. More than once, he had felt Stacion snatching power from him at an inconvenient time. Only his hidden reserve had saved him.

"What bothers you, daughter?" Larcia's 'voice' reached Jai.

Jai stopped running the now smooth and polished stones through her fingers. The spell that had tumbled them had been left active for many weeks – powered by a tendril of the aura of Korvu.

"I am no closer to thinking of a way to make Stacion Ansuni see reason," Jai phrased her discontent. "The Kumatan are nibbling at our borders and the other tribes are openly challenging him – and always he is angry – and he isn't answering the challenges."

"His restraint is so far commendable," Larcia commented. "What would you have him do?"

Jai thought about how he had retaliated in the past and shuddered. She didn't like what he had done before. She shrugged, "I'm not sure, but Con said he talks of challenging all the tribes at once. But surely that would take more power than even he could command."

Larcia's voice was silent for a time. "It is the lesser sorcerers that have challenged him so far. By not reacting to their challenges, he shows his contempt of them. The older ones are more cautious. They will be slower to act – but if they do – Stacion will have to react."

"But how can he possibly take them all at once?" Jai asked.

Another silence. "Only by such an action as to also cause massive destruction. He would destroy his own tribe as well."

"That's what I thought," Jai said. "He must be mad to consider it."

"You should try to see if he is storing power in artefacts – relics. He might also be able to draw life energy from his tribe. He could draw on the aura, but I don't sense that. The other sorcerers and that Kumatan traegers would sense that too, and that could lead them to the tribe."

"Is the power of the Kumatan like ours?" Jai asked.

"All power comes from the aura. We, the Atapi are closest to it. The Kumatan seem to have lost the knowledge of where their power comes from and they use what they have in a different way."

That idea was new to Jai, but it didn't seem to help her problem. Another idea held more interest.

"Could I make a power relic?" she asked Larcia.

"Yes, but the aura is yours to use. What reasons have you to need one?"

A vague notion was all she had. "For now, I'd like to understand how to make one and how they work," Jai told Larcia. "Perhaps to learn how to trigger the power in one."

"That could be dangerous," Larcia warned.

"I'll learn that too," Jai admitted.

"Very well," Larcia considered. "Next time you come, bring a box or a drinking vessel or something made of bone or metal. Metal is better. It doesn't need to be big."

"What is a box?" Jai asked. A picture formed in her mind of a metal object that opened at the top and was only big enough to hold a few of her smooth rocks.

"Where would I get metal for something like that?"

Another picture came into her mind. It was of a sunlit glade in the shadow of a mountain, near a waterfall.

"What is that place?" Jai marvelled.

"Forgotten land," Larcia seemed to sigh. "There is no tribe there now."

"What happened?"

"The tribe died out," Larcia said. "Like many others. There were dozens of tribes, once. Now I sense only twenty. But there is metal there. The tribe once made fine jewellery and metal things. I will teach you how they brought metal to the surface."

"I have never heard of such a thing," Jai admitted. "Our artisans must use metal stolen from Kumatan or others. How will I find it?"

"I will teach you," Larcia promised. "You can read what has been known before."

Jai was keen to learn, but a wry thought in her mind made her smile. It seemed that for everything she wanted to know – there was a flurry of other things she needed to learn first. And she had the feeling that she was running out of time.

The Elder Mother summoned all the women at a time when the village was almost completely deserted by the males. Only the few wounded males and those males too old to fight, or the artisans remained and they kept well away from the women.

The children were all grouped under the watchful eyes of two ancient mothers.

Jai stayed towards the back of the group of women, distancing herself from the idea she had proposed to her elders. Every female, she had suggested, should learn to fight – to defend herself, other women and her children. They had agreed, recalling their own training - skills that had not been taught for a long time. They had tested Jai, and were pleased by her skill.

The expected outcry from the pampered mates of the strongest warriors was echoed by many others.

The Elder Mother, with remorseless logic, broke down their resistance. "Times like now, when our warriors are often out fighting those who intrude on our land, when we alone are left to defend the heart of out tribe – should we let ourselves die if an intruder sneaks here? Should we let them kill our children?"

"But our Esteemed leader protects us here," a young woman cried out.

"What one sorcerer can create, another can negate," an old women remarked.

The group was silenced. They all knew that danger lurked outside the village. Some instinctively felt for their hunting knives. They had grown used to having warriors accompany them on foraging parties to protect them.

"Teach us, Elder Mother," was the unanimous cry.

Jai marvelled as the Elder Mother demonstrated the moves of a defensive dance. She recognized moves that Con had taught her. As one of many, Jai practiced moves she already knew. She watched Bernea learn with intense concentration, saw Siluci, sullen at first, become pleased with her own skill. Jai wondered if Siluci realised the true nature of the dance.

The older women noticed when Jai edged out of the group, but made no reference to it. They saw her reach the stand of trees that separated this area from that of the unmated warriors. They did not see her walk forward and vanish.

The waterfall tinkled peacefully as Jai arrived. She stopped to listen to it and heard other sounds. What she heard was the unworried sounds of birds, animals and insects. She sniffed the air, marvelling how different it was to the she normally breathed. It was fresher, purer. She wondered at the difference.

This land, Larcia had said, had been deserted for two centuries and shunned by other tribes. Some unknown disaster had killed all the tribe that had once lived here. Larcia, for all her age and wisdom, did not know the truth only that for a long time an alien taint had lingered.

Jai, standing still, sensed no danger. She began to move around, letting her mind sink into the aura — to sense the "feel" of metal as Larcia had taught her. As she began to sense metal, some other power began to stir, and Jai began to feel the pull of magic. Con had mentioned this, and she had felt the pull of the magic objects in her sire's relic cave. That pull had made her feel dirty, this pull attracted her.

The pull, of magic, drew her into a cave behind the waterfall. Enough light filtered through the water to show her the stone altar and the objects on it. Without touching them, she walked around, until she came to the bones of a winged Atapi, resting against the back wall.

The sorcerer, dead so long ago, was still guarding his land. Jai felt, for a moment, that the bones would stir and attack her. For once in her life she was afraid. Her mind called to Larcia.

The sense of the ancient one filled her mind.

"Loschak," Larcia said, naming the dead sorcerer. "Like you, of the line of Socon. Touch the bones, daughter."

Jai moved forward, slowly reaching out from arm's length away. At first, nothing happened, and then pictures began to form I her mind. Some power held her immobile.

As clear as if she were there, Jai saw a thriving community, felt the pride of Loschak as he surveyed it. Then she felt anger and saw another sorcerer appear, and she heard the unrefusable challenge.

The ensuing battle lasted three days, but was compressed into flashing images seen from Loschak's eyes. Both sorcerers sustained near fatal injuries, both were almost bereft of power, neither would give in; neither had achieved a substantive advantage.

The Tribe's warriors, drove off the interloper, followed him to the edge of their lands. Loschak crawled into his cave to recover.

In a corner of her mind, Jai wondered why he had not called on the aura to help him heal.

Time had passed, but not many days, when the still weak sorcerer sensed danger. He left his cave, only to see before him strangers. They were not Atapi or Kumatan, or even Kimh. They smelled like nothing on Korvu. Before he could issue a challenge, they raised their arms and from an object in their hands – fire and metal flew.

Jai felt the pain, felt her body experience the shock of the injury. She had sensed such phantom pain before when healing, and as then banished it.

Loschak lay helpless, able only to stare at the sky. His mind was unable to shape the magic to destroy the strangers. His strength and will came back slowly as the aura passively healed him. But by then it was too late. The strangers had killed the tribe. All of them – down to the smallest of the babies.

For a moment, all Loschak wanted to do was die in shame, but then his thoughts turned to recall that some of his tribe still lived in those who had chosen to go with his son to found a new tribe. Fear for his son gave him the strength to crawl back into his cave to consider ways to rid Korvu of these alien killers.

First he used all his powers to learn about them. He watched what they did by scrying in a bowl of water. He saw that they were stealing metals from the ground.

His mind stored every detail, and later he recorded it onto a metal box, etched with a stylus of wind. The runes included to trigger a vision of what he had seen.

As he watched and planned, his mind harvested power from the aura. The energy there, from his dead tribe, formed his revenge.

The twelve arrogant strangers, who had left him for dead, looked up from their labours and saw the Atapi sorcerer – seemingly twelve feet tall, striding towards them with his wings fully extended.

Their weapons once again spat fire and metal, but this time they had no effect. The aliens scattered, only to run into swarms of tiny whirlwinds. The aliens shrieked as the flesh was shredded into a bluish pulp, each glob of their odd coloured flesh burst into flame as it touched the ground.

The fleshless skeletons dropped, one by one, and burst into flame.

The whirlwinds slowed and the energy dispersed.

Loschak sent a call to his fellow sorcerers, but the call went unanswered. He walked back to his cave, lay his knife next to the box on the altar, stirred a tiny wind to etch the last memories and sat down to wait the judgement due to a sorcerer who let his tribe die.

Even then, he didn't know he was already dead.

Chapter 13

Jai jerked her hand free, feeling sickened. Not only because of what happened to the tribe, but because it had been Stacion Ansuni who had fought Loschak. And also because one of the aliens had worn a decorated hare's pelt, such as Stacion had worn in the earlier visions.

"Daughter, bring the box and the knife – bring them to me. This is something that must be shared by all."

Larcia's voice in her head cleared Jai's mind of the horror she had been shown. She obeyed the command, no longer wanting to mine metal in this place. She went at once, knowing that even as she walked to the Rock of Arkor, that Stacion was challenging another sorcerer, even as Con kept the Kumatan busy.

Her dreaming cave had an aura of peace that Jai allowed to flow through her mind.

"Come through to me, daughter," Larcia invited after giving Jai time to regain her inner peace.

Jai was surprised to see an opening in the back wall where none had been before. She went to it, not afraid, only curious. The short tunnel led to another cave – this one with a stone altar, like to the one in the waterfall cave.

Jai placed the box there with the knife.

"The knife is yours, daughter," Larcia told her.

"But…I'm not a sorcerer, and that's a sorcerer's knife." Jai argued, even as her hand was closing on the hilt.

"What did you think of the place you saw," Larcia asked.

"It was beautiful, pure and clean," Jai said. "I cannot see why another tribe did not claim it."

"Because tradition holds that once such a tragedy has happened there – it can again," Larcia explained.

"That's stupid. I sensed nothing dangerous there."

"If no sorcerer would go there – can you see an advantage to you?"

"Refuge," Jai said immediately. "But I couldn't live there alone. The tribe needs me."

"You share common blood with Loschak, you have his knife. His lands, by tradition are yours."

"Do you mean – if Stacion had managed to take this knife, back then, He would have won tribe and land?"

"That is the tradition," Larcia agreed. "And you recognised your sire?"

"Yes, and I saw his fancy hare's pelt on one of those alien beasts. He has another one like it that he wears when he wants to be imposing. I wonder what his reward was for leaving that place unprotected and why he didn't go back later and take that land. And don't say tradition, because he knew what happened there."

"That may be true, but maybe those aliens scared him," Larcia suggested.

Jai snorted. "No, I don't think so. Perhaps seeing the burnt and pulped flesh did – if he thought Loschak dead – he probably didn't know what had killed the aliens and expected the same to happen to him."

"Perhaps that is the truth," Larcia allowed.

"With this knife – would I have to become a sorcerer?"

"No. You could, however, challenge the other sorcerers and if you won, they would have to accept you."

"Could I give this knife away? Would the new owner then take the lands for his own?"

"If you chose," Larcia agreed. "A sorcerer makes his knife when he becomes a sorcerer. It stays with him, always. He can pass it to a chosen successor, though it is done rarely. Few sorcerers live to die of old age."

"So would this knife still contain the essence of Loschak?" Jai asked.

"Yes," Larcia confirmed. "But you need not fear it."

"I think it would serve Con better than me. He will challenge Stacion one day. Perhaps if the essence of Loschak still lingers in it, there will be a hidden advantage. It has already tasted Stacion's blood. If I could get close enough to him with a weapon, I would try to kill him myself without warning. He cannot see magic in me – and doesn't see me as a threat, that way – but fire and metal can kill just as dead."

"Do you consider that honourable?" Larcia questioned.

Jai considered, and answered truthfully even though fearing Larcia's disapproval. "No, but I think that Stacion discarded honour two centuries before I was born. Nothing that Con has told me lets me believe he has found it again. If he keeps on as he is, I fear for my tribe. He is not so far gone as to discard his powerbase, his people, but he even draws from the aura power that they need to heal. And, with Kumatan and all the other sorcerers against him – he is surely courting disaster and too arrogant to see it."

"Do you understand why this cannot be?" Larcia asked.

"For my tribe, yes. But, for the others, I suppose that if the sorcerers are busy trying to get at Stacion, they are not protecting their tribes and the power they are wasting could be put to better use."

"All that is true," Larcia agreed. "Without the sorcerers, the tribes are weak. What else?"

Jai thought, but all her mind could produce were the teachings she had learnt about obeying the tribe's leader, the sorcerer. She idly turned the knife over, and suddenly the horror returned.

"Could those aliens return? Have they?"

"They have come once. They know we are here. I cannot sense any taint, but if the tribes wage war on each other…"

"They could come without anyone to stop them…" Jai finished. "What of the Kumatan? Do they know of these aliens?"

"I do not know. But although the Kumatan will fight, they are not a warlike race, nor are the Kimh." Larcia explained.

"So we – the Atapi – must be prepared to protect all," Jai asked.

"Which is the way it should be," Larcia stated. "Though it is not what tradition has become. Your instincts are good, daughter."

Jai gave a derisive laugh. "Stacion would consider that idea to be heresy and treason. He considers Kumatan as prey."

As Jai began to form another question, she felt an urgent call in her mind. It wasn't Con, and it wasn't Stacion, nor was it the ancient one, though there was something familiar about it.

"I must go," Jai said aloud. She did not make her normal respectful withdrawal before walking back across plains to the tribe's village.

The women were racing from their sacred grove as Jai returned. In that first instant back, she understood the urgent call that had caused her to return so precipitously.

Con! Con was mortally injured. He could not have called her, but she shared blood with him, had shared a womb with him. Their life energies were linked with each other – in a way that few would guess.

Six warriors surrounded the litter that four of them had carried back. All ten bore wounds of their own, yet they had ignored them, for Con's sake.

"Bring water and cloth," Jai called to two young Atapi as she too raced towards the litter. She knew that the healers would bring their herbs and salves.

The warriors lowered the litter and moved to let her near Con. Two of the younger warriors eyed her with respect. They had benefitted from her skill.

Con wasn't conscious. His wounds were deep and oozed blood. Jai began working with practiced actions. She would not let Con die!

Until the cloths arrived, she could not bind his wounds, but she could still try to stop the bleeding. Using magic that she had learnt as an incidental side effect to a sorcerer's spell, she drew the aura into her and concentrated on her hands. Her hands became hot and she placed them on a bleeding wound. The heat dried the blood, forming a scab. She moved to the next, and the next.

Bernea moved beside her with the water and cloths. An older woman had the healing herbs and salves. They cleansed around the delicate scabs and applied the herbals before binding each wound.

Jai placed a hand on Con's forehead and one on the ground and drew on the aura to help him heal.

He felt to her senses like an almost dead husk. The energy that she was used to sensing in him was at low ebb. She worked to fill the void.

"What happened," Jai asked the surrounding warriors, but without looking at them. They all kept their eyes outward, watching for danger. One answered, but he too did not look at her. He was not meant to talk to her, or acknowledge her; he would claim to be answering one of the other women.

"The Kumatan anticipated our ambush. Master Con had planned that. The enemy wasn't a Traeger, but he was more skilled with a sword than most of our enemies. Con was playing with him, when the sun darkened. Master Con seemed to stumble, and did not see the enemy coming at him. That enemy seemed surprised at his success. We drew our weapons then, to protect Master Con. The enemy had not seen us until then, and he turned to flee in the face of our superior force. He had others with him, and these fought us instead, but we proved to be the stronger and they fled soon after."

Jai vaguely wondered why that Kumatan hadn't finished the job and killed Con. It would have taken only moments. Con should not have been hurt. He was, in spite of hiding his skills from Stacion, every bit as skilled as the warriors and probably better than any Kumatan. What had made him vulnerable?

"Did you notice anything about the sun, Bernea?" Jai asked. It might have been a local phenomenon, but in any case, Jai, had been in the Rock of Arkor.

"Yes," Bernea whispered. "It seemed like a cloud crossed the sun, but there were no clouds and in that moment, I felt weak."

Bernea suddenly grabbed Jai's arm – and in that moment, the sun's brightness dimmed again. Jai glanced around. Bernea slumped over Con and the old woman sat abruptly on the ground. The warriors looked ready to fall down too. She could feel her power being dragged from her and suddenly she knew.

"Stak – there is no more power here for you," Jai whispered fiercely. The power dragging stopped. Jai risked a passive glimpse of Stacion's mind.

Stacion was fighting a young sorcerer, and if he had to drag power from Con and anyone in his tribe with sensitivity to magic – then his opponent was one to be wary of.

While seeming to be using her healing skill to help Con, Jai muttered the words that let her listen to Stacion's thoughts without him sensing her.

She endured the language that he was using to distract his opponent. It was meant to enrage him and it was succeeding. Stacion had no thoughts of being defeated. He was too confident of his own power. The young sorcerer was equally confident of his own skills – against such an aged devil.

The wounds on the young sorcerer attested to Stacion's skill with his knife, yet Stacion was tiring, or he would not need quick energy – life energy.

Jai directed her attention through Stacion's eyes and watched closely. The younger sorcerer still had plenty of energy, but where was he getting it from? Stacion would have blocked him from the aura, one of his favourite strategies. So where? Jai closed her mental eyes and sensed the energy flows through Stacion. The energy drain was as clear as if it was water flowing downhill. The energy was flowing from Stacion, through the opponent's knife and into the young sorcerer. It was a clever ploy, but how was he doing it?

She felt Con's mind waking and hushed him. He spoke softly, letting her know he was aware of what she was receiving.

"It's a leech blade," Con told her. "Like a star blade. It must have nicked him, and then returned to the thrower. It only needs a trace of his blood to work. The bastard grabbed at my power and made me vulnerable, but without me, the Kumatan will sense this battle."

"Serve him right," Jai murmured.

"But he will blame me – possibly kill me," Con murmured in return.

"He won't kill you - he still needs you. You are smarter than Lancho and I am sure he knows it."

"I don't feel it!"

"And I doubt he will admit it to you."

Jai concentrated again on Stacion's thoughts and knew Con was sharing them. She felt the surge of anger when Stacion sensed the Kumatan. It was the rage of a predator being deprived of its prey.

"He can't fight both that whelp and the Kumatan," Con murmured. "And he won't walk out of this fight – he'd lose face. He must see that the whelp is matching him."

"Should we do anything?" Jai asked Con. "The Kumatan can have them both."

"If the Kumatan kill our Sire, every other landless sorcerer will come here to fight for the tribe's lands," Con predicted.

Jai frowned, but an idea came to her mind. Con shared it and with a faint smile, he nodded that he agreed that it would work. Jai closed her eyes, to concentrate better and whispered the words that would let her nudge Stacion's mind unnoticed. She imaged a picture of the younger Atapi being thrown onto the Kumatan swords. Stacion embraced the idea, believing it was his own.

The passive observer in his mind saw him wait until the younger Atapi became aware of the Kumatan, and in that instant of distraction used his dwindling energy to toss his rival at them. Even as he released the other Atapi, Stacion walked forward to return to his tribe.

Chapter 14

"So, he's got out of a losing fight with his arrogance unscathed," Con growled softly.

Jai removed her watch on Stacion's mind as the old woman seemed to materialise beside her.

"Hide that knife, daughter," the woman ordered. Jai realised that she had dropped Loschak's knife in plain view and Stacion was striding towards them. The woman hid her movement as she tucked the knife under Con.

"What is my apprentice doing, bleeding all over the place," Stacion accused, but his voice sounded smug, not angry.

"Master, a misjudgement," Con admitted. "When you wanted power, I gave freely, but the Kumatan warrior attacked at that moment. My warriors gave me time to draw from the aura and then we forced him to flee."

"You don't need magic to use a sword," Stacion growled.

"No, but by pretending to be weak, he came too close. He misjudged. He did not expect me to know how to use one."

Stacion bared his teeth in approval. "Come when these tyrannical women release you."

Con waited until Stacion was well away before giving an audible sigh. He tried to sit up, but had to flop back. He pointed to Jai and Bernea and ordered, "You and you, bring food and drink to my cave."

To the warriors, he said, "Take me to somewhere more private."

The warriors hefted the litter and Con lay back, still with the knife under him.

Jai whispered to Bernea as the trotted to obey Con's order. "I'll get the food. Could you see if you can find where Stacion went?"

Bernea trotted in a different direction, but soon joined Jai at the communal cooking area.

"He went to one of the artisans and told him to turn something into a knife," Bernea told Jai. "Then he went into his cave, calling for Siluci."

Jai smirked. "Then we will have a little time. Can you take the food to Con? I'll prepare a second carrier for Stacion. No doubt, Siluci will be arriving soon to get food for him."

Jai worked slowly until Bernea was out of sight, then finished quickly. When no one was paying attention to her, she slipped away to where the artisans worked. Only one male was there and he was blowing a small stream of air into a brazier.

"Laguno," Jai greeted the old man.

"Hei!" he replied paying only slight attention to her. "What do you want?"

"I heard Stacion gave you metal for a knife," Jai said quickly. "For a knife worthy of our leader – you would need jewels for the hilt. Have you any? Or could I help you find some?"

Laguno stopped blowing air to study her. "He likes red and purple."

Jai nodded. "What did he give you?"

Laguno merely gestured with his hand towards his small anvil. Jai moved only enough to see the star shaped blade and the traces of purple blood on it. Con had been correct, though Jai had not seen Stacion take it from his rival.

Laguno turned his head away from her, but asked, "Should I wash the blood from it first?"

Ideas came into Jai's mind, drawn from things she had read about in the aura of Korvu.

"Did Stacion say anything?" Jai asked.

Laguno shook his head.

"Then, no. The flames will burn it clean," Jai told him. Laguno nodded, and Jai slipped away as if she had never been there.

Jai was back at the food area when Siluci stormed into get food for her mate. Jai indicated the second carrier as she lifted the food and drink for Con. Siluci's face lost some of its resentment and she refrained from her usual insults. Jai said nothing as she headed back to Con's cave, making sure she was making enough noise to be heard approaching.

From Bernea's blush, Jai knew she had just sprung away from Con. She made no comment, but was inwardly glad that Con seemed to be returning Bernea's interest.

"Ber? I forgot to get the hare's milk. Will you go get it?"

Bernea sensed that Jai needed to talk to Con, and went off without complaint.

"Put up a shield," Jai said softly. Con knew she meant for him to block Stacion from eaves- dropping on his thoughts.

"Didn't you have your power blocked from him?" Jai demanded.

"Yes, but he took it at the worst moment," Con told her. "What I had left, I used to help the warriors who carried me back. If I hadn't, we would all have died." His mind quickly reviewed the true action, not the fable he had told Stacion.

"Was the one you fought a Traeger?"

"It is possible that it was a young one," Con considered. "He was testing himself against me, and I against him. I won. Now, what is that knife you put under me? It is pulling oddly on my senses."

"It belonged to a sorcerer named Loschak. It is two centuries old. Larcia said it was mine, as were his lands. I give it to you."

Con searched his memory. "That is shunned land."

"Yes," Jai admitted. "But I was there. I saw what happened there when I touched Loschak's bones. He made a record, that I was led to and which Larcia now has. Next time you go to the rock, seek the knowledge. But what is important is that the knife does not like Stacion Ansuni."

"Did he have some part in that matter?" Con asked and Jai nodded. "But if he killed Loschak, he'd hold those lands."

"He critically weakened Loschak, not the rest," Jai stated.

"Why give me the land?" Con asked. "Larcia said it was yours."

"What is mine – is yours. Anyway – think on it. What would it mean if you challenge Stacion and win or he agrees to split the tribe."

"He will never agree to that," Con stated positively.

"Then you do it," Jai suggested bluntly. "There are those who would follow you without hesitation. If they vanished, one by one over time – to a place where no one goes – everyone will blame the encroaching sorcerers or the Kumatan."

Con's eyes began to gleam as he considered the audacious idea. "Yes, and this knife – I'll make it seem like a trophy from a foolish Kumatan and too poor looking to attract his attention."

Jai nodded agreement. "One other thing. He got the star blade from that sorcerer he was tormenting. He told Laguno to turn it into a knife. I told Laguno that the fire will clean the blade of Stacion's blood and I will find gems to decorate the hilt and sheath."

"A leech blade – wouldn't that still benefit him?"

"Perhaps – but it has tasted his blood – what if someone used it on him?"

Con considered. "Do you know?"

"Not for sure but with his blood bonded to it – it might drain him – give another an unexpected advantage."

"Womb-mate – I am glad you are not my enemy," Con said with appreciation. "I cannot assume that will be the case, but having jewels attuned to us on the hilt – yes – that would help. You must be careful – Stacion might sense your meddling."

"I will be as careful as always. He might be surprised that I want to make it impressive for him. He will believe it's his due and disregard me as usual. I will show the stones to the Elder Mothers and have them teach me how to bind a healing spell onto them and that is what I will tell Laguno."

"Devious," Con acknowledged. "And as he will not let any other use it – he won't realise that it will heal others too?"

Jai snorted. "I had better go – but don't forget – you are welcome at the Rock – any time – Larcia said so. You can go and dream dreams of knowledge – if you think about what you want to know."

"Without my Master?" Con savoured the idea. "I have no chance to get away."

That was only too true, but Jai had a suggestion. "Put a glamour on Siluci – so she can keep him busy all night."

Con snorted, just as Bernea returned.

"He's all yours," Jai told her friend as she left.

Next morning, Jai overheard Bernea talking to the Eldest Mother, saying that Con was feverish and claiming that the Kumatan he had fought must have poisoned his knife. For an instant, Jai was worried, then Bernea turned slightly, grinned and shoulder gestured to indicate that Siluci was listening.

The Elder Mother glanced at Jai, her message was clear. "You are not needed." The old woman understood what was needed and should Stacion check – the knife would indeed have faint traces of poison on it. The healers would keep Stacion away from Con, if the sorcerer's own abhorrence of being sick did not.

The Elder Mother seemed to notice Jai and asked brusquely why she was there.

"We are short of some herbs," Jai stated, naming several, and let the Elder guess that she wanted to be away from the tribe.

"You are the best at finding them," the Elder agreed. "Don't go alone! Wait!"

The old woman trotted past a screen of bushes. She could be heard ordering two warriors to "Get off your lazy backsides and do some work. Your wounds are nothing and if Jai didn't get more herbs there would be none the next time they needed healing."

Jai was relieved when the two warriors emerged, settling their weapons. Both were already grateful to her for her healing of them. Neither spoke to her or paid particular attention to her, but simply followed her out of the camp in the direction of the woods.

Once out of the camp they stayed alert and let her lead the way. They stood watch as she moved in and out of the cover of trees, seeking the herbs she wanted.

When she had enough herbs to be convincing, she gestured for the warriors to follow her and she trotted to an open, sunlit rock outcrop.

"Keep back a bit," she directed the warriors. "I have some woman's magic to do on the herbs."

They listened, but gave her no reaction.

It was an advantage to being almost ignored. They wouldn't ask her questions as to why she chose that particular place. She had reasons ready, but the truth was that she knew that there was metal beneath the ground at that spot.

Jai began a ritual to increase the potency of the herbs. It was a test, to see if Stacion Ansuni would react.

He did, arriving abruptly. He arrived in front of her where he would see the different herbs arranged in a careful star shape.

"Your skills are increasing," he commented and his voice had a dangerous edge to it.

Jai stopped chanting. "Thank you, Majestic One," she bowed her head and studied her folded knees. "The Old Mothers will tell me if I have done well enough when I return. They tell me that this ritual works best in untouched land – closer to the aura."

Stacion glared at her bent head as if searching her mind for deceit. But Jai had been prepared for him and her mind gave him only her recitation of the ritual and her fear she would get it wrong.

Jai watched Stacion's bare feet and saw them turn abruptly and vanish. Without disturbing the herbs, Jai overturned the small bowl that had gone unremarked at the centre of the star and began a new chant. Even if Stacion checked again, he'd only hear the other chant.

The sense of the aura flowed into Jai with familiar ease. She felt with her mind for the sense of "metal" in its crude state. She sensed 'copper' the same metal that Loschak had used for his box. She summoned the metal by imagining it flowing from the rock bed where it lay, through fine cracks in the rock and into the upended bowl where it was to coalesce with only like matter.

When the bowl was full, she ended the chant. The metal in the bowl stayed there, the rest slipped back into the rock. Whilst the metal hardened, Jai resumed the herb chant. It would not be wise to have neglected her reason for being away from the village. Stacion would be sure to check. He would want to know if she was becoming powerful. He had never sensed her potential – but he knew very well who had sired her. And being Stacion Ansuni – he was paranoid about controlling all the power he could.

The Elder Mothers had never doubted her potential. They knew how important it was to the tribe. They never talked of it – for that would have been a death sentence for her. So they trained her to heal – an important and prized skill, but never admitted how skilled she was. Nor would they betray her now. If asked the Elder Mothers would only say that her skill was 'adequate' not 'exceptional'.

After carefully stowing the herbs into separate bundles in her waist pouch, Jai told the warriors that she needed to range further for other medicinal plants. Neither questioned her, nor complained when she asked them to help her up to reach fungi growing high on tree trunks. Both obeyed readily when she stopped them from following her into a thicket of brambles.

Neither realised that for a time they were guarding no one. Jai used the cover to 'walk' across planes to the Rock of Arkor.

Chapter 15

In her cave, Jai thought a greeting to Larcia and felt her welcome.

"I am pleased that your brother came to me," Larcia told Jai. "He is bright and full of promise. A joy – like you."

"Thank you, my Queen," Jai said, sincerely. "I'm glad too, though with Lancho who knows where – Con can't get away much."

"Perhaps you should rekindle your friendship with the Kumatan girl," Larcia suggested.

"I have no wish to be trapped again by her father," Jai admitted. "He is not well disposed towards us."

"With reason, but also with prejudice," Larcia admitted. "But such a contact could yield rich rewards."

"I would like to see Suzi again, but I think her father sent her from their house. Twice I have tried to see her in her place but that place is not lived in now."

"If her father, the Traeger, felt they were in danger, then perhaps you should seek her amongst the Kimh. Those that claim to rule this world," Larcia suggested.

Jai refrained from wondering if Larcia was 'mad' to suggest going near the race that the mere mention of made Atapi quiver.

"Surely, if Suzi were there – the security would be much stronger," Jai asked, her tone carefully neutral.

"I am not insane," Larcia assured her. "They are creatures, no better or worse than Kumatan or Atapi – just different. They cannot sense the aura like we can and Traegers can. However, even though I cannot sense within their palace – there gardens are not blocked from the aura."

Jai understood what she implied. "Have you a picture of that place?"

Larcia only said, "You will have to work out a way to get there."

Jai put the idea aside to think about. Her sense of time nudged her to do what she had come for. She found her tumbling rocks and stilled the magic. They were all beautifully polished. From amongst the colourful rocks she pulled out a number of red and purple ones – each about the same size. These went into her belt pouch under the herbs. She would have to do the magic on them later – so that the stones would always recognise her. She hoped to make the knife they adorned skitter away from harming her.

"You are very clever little daughter," Larcia said in Jai's mind, making her jump.

"Are you angry with me?" Jai asked, realising that Larcia had read her thoughts. That the old sorceress had realised that she was planning on creating a weapon to kill the sorcerer of her tribe.

"It is the tradition for younger sorcerers to challenge the old. It is to strengthen the tribes."

"But I am a female!" Jai stated.

"So am I,' Larcia countered.

Jai swallowed any other protest. "I have to go."

"Daughter, it would be better if you yourself worked the metal. The magic would be stronger."

Jai mentally agreed to the advice and quickly returned to the bramble patch she had left. She heard the warriors calling her and hastened out — allowing thorns to scratch her.

Jai delivered the herbs to the Elder Mothers as soon as she returned. While she waited for them to evaluate her work, she saw Siluci sidling closer and wondered who was watching her whelp. Atapi babies became mobile very early.

Siluci, while appearing not to be listening would hear everything that the Mothers said to her and no doubt report it to Stacion. Jai hoped so for then any paranoid fears he had would be removed again — for a while.

Jai slipped away as soon as she could whilst Siluci asked for salves to cleanse and heal scratches on her son. Some of that would be useful on herself, Jai thought, but a wash in cool water would do as well. Especially if she wanted to be noticed sporting bramble scratches. She'd been gone longer than planned and the two warriors had been worried when she had finally answered their quiet calls. The scratches had removed any faint suspicions in their minds.

In the unmated women's cavern, Bernea intercepted Jai. "Can you bring some food and go to Con?"

"Yes," Jai agreed without asking why. If Con was back from where she knew he had been — perhaps he had something important to say.

Jai took a loaded tray to Con's cave, where Bernea was sitting outside the entrance. The two girls smiled at each other. Bernea knew that Jai was not a rival for Con's affections.

Con was sitting on his sleeping pad and looking much improved. In fact, he looked elated. Jai sensed his excitement.

"I have…" he began.

"Hush," Jai warned. Con nodded and when he finished it was in a whisper.

"My name," Con finished.

Jai gripped his arms, sharing his delight.

"I didn't think it was possible. I am not even a score of years old."

"Don't doubt your worth," Jai advised. "Nor think it makes you omnipotent. You still have much to learn, but it is both a weapon and a protection."

"Never fear," Con assured her. "I will use it with caution. But now – now – I can begin to select my tribe. You'll be one – won't you?"

"Did you doubt? I'll stay at your side forever."

They gripped hands, sealing the promise.

"One more thing…" Con pulled something from his waist pouch. Colourful stones dropped into her palm. "Bound to me – as those other you made are bound to you. Larcia gave them to me."

"She read my mind and approved," Jai admitted. "And I guess that they will be the only ascension present you are likely to get."

Con snorted. "I doubt that I would want Stacion's present."

Jai grinned and hid the stones in her pouch and left to consider where to do the ritual on her stones.

Jai hid her crude copper ingot and most of her stones in a cave that overlooked the village. Now that she had protected it with a ritual to make people forget about it – her secret things would be safe enough in their hiding place. She had thought to take them to her dreaming cave – but felt that the time was not right to leave the village.

It wasn't exactly a feeling of danger – just of unease. She felt like there was a storm building, but the skies were clear.

She glanced down and saw Stacion pacing around the village, glancing around and sniffing as if he too sensed something. Con had been sent to check further afield – in other parts of the tribe's land. He had been gone for hours.

Jai sat down outside her cave and allowed herself to feel the aura. The feeling of unease intensified. The aura felt wrong – as if it were being warped for some purpose. She sought for the source of the wrongness. It seemed to be somewhere across the river, just off the tribe's land. For an instant, she felt as if she had touched a mind and had a glimpse of inky black clouds amassing over a range of low hills and the sense that the rain would be deadly.

She reached for Con's mind, forgetting to shield her own. She showed him the picture. Below her, Stacion turned to stare at her and then at the hills. He began bellowing orders – for everyone to get into rock covered shelter.

Con materialised then, as if summoned by Stacion.

"Whoever is doing this is across the river," Con said and his voice carried. "I can't see him but he is pulling the aura from this area. Every creature is silent. Master – have you any idea what he is doing?"

For once, Stacion didn't ignore the question. "Several. None pleasant. One is a burning rain, another is a rain of poisonous snakes, and another is a poisonous wind. We need to add shields over the village. I will have to have your help as Lancho is not here."

Con dared a suggestion. "Master, if you need more help – call the healers. Their power is slight but if you realise how healing is done, they know what is 'right' and what is 'wrong'. They can boost your efforts to fight this thing that is approaching as it is clearly wrong."

Stacion stared at Con for a moment, but issued the summons. The female healers raced to him and listened to what he directed. They raced off to their healing circle – all except Jai.

Jai had as little choice in responding as the others, but Stacion glared at her as if she were not welcome.

"I felt your mind, woman! You sensed something across the river."

"Yes," Jai admitted. "Just for an instant. Was that the enemy?"

"Whoever he is – I want him. If you can sense him – you can find him."

It was an order that she couldn't disobey – even if obeying could mean her death. Not when her tribe's sorcerer added that implacable coercion. Not when she herself realised that the life of her whole tribe was at stake.

But how did he expect her to capture this unknown creature? She wasn't a warrior. All she had was a belt knife for protection. Still, she had no choice and began running towards the river – towards the strongest sense of 'wrongness'. She was relieved when she realised that several warriors had begun to race after her. More so when she realised that each of those warriors was well disposed towards her.

Before she reached the river, Jai slowed to approach more cautiously.

"I cannot see any one," one of the warriors said very softly. The others were scanning the area and sniffing.

Jai could only see the intruder as an area of glowing light. "A sorcerer. He's standing just to the left of the cairn that marks the crossing point."

It was a mark of respect that the warriors didn't question her.

"Stacion wants him alive," Jai stated. "And if he is expecting anything other than the results of his vile sorcery it will be a magical retaliation. I'll give him one."

The elder of the warriors with her said softly, "He will laugh at you. He will not consider you dangerous."

Jai grinned briefly. "And while he is laughing – he won't expect a physical attack!"

The warriors all snarled softly, appreciating her tactic. They spread out and began to encircle the stranger with the intent of capturing him.

Jai knew that she had been seen as soon as she started crossing the river. Before then she had already invoked Larcia's protection and felt the ancient one's disgust at what this young sorcerer was doing.

The sorcerer stayed in his position, but the pulling in the aura eased – as he considered her.

Knowing that Stacion was aware of her actions, through her open mind, Jai began to chant a ritual for healing. To her surprise, she felt the energies being worked by the sorcerer, eddying away from his control. It took a while for the arrogant worm to notice.

"So – Stacion Ansuni sends a female to do his work?" the sorcerer taunted and became visible. "He hides behind women."

Feeling Stacion's anger in her mind, Jai retorted quickly, "Your pitiful sorcery is beneath his dignity to notice. After all, if one has a suppurating wound, one calls a healer, not a master sorcerer?"

Jai sensed the anger of the young sorcerer and was not surprised when a bolt of energy was flung at her. She didn't try to dodge. Instead she trusted to Larcia's protection and watched as the energy dissipated in a shower of sparks, inches away from her.

The sorcerer stalked closer to her. "I will have you!"

"Will you?" Jai asked, noticing the warriors closing in. She began chanting again and felt the energies changing. The sorcerer returned to his own ritual, but kept watching her. That was his mistake. A spear flew from the hand of a warrior and impaled him.

Several things happened at once. Jai felt the sorcerer's name come into her mind and she felt the energies he had sent out returning – followed by Stacion's anger.

The warriors were close around Jai and their victim. Just in time, Jai created a bubble of protection.

What impacted her protection was a rain of tiny snakes, no longer than a hand span in length. They sizzled against the barrier, before falling to the ground at the edge of the barrier. The energy that created them was making a lightning storm around them.

Jai would have attempted to return the energy to the aura, but that would have betrayed her mastery of magic. So she waited, expecting Stacion to come for his prisoner.

Through her barrier, she saw Con arrive first. He saw the slither snakes and sent swathes of flame at them. When the immediate area was clear, Stacion arrived, looking well pleased. No doubt he was taking into himself the wild returning energies. Finally he walked over to her and destroyed her protecting shield with a wave of his hand and a quick mental phrase.

"How – did you learn to do that?" Stacion demanded.

Jai knew what he meant. "Majestic one – it is a healer's spell – to keep infection away from an injured patient. Women's magic – no more."

"You were unexpectedly smart to think of that," Stacion praised, though his face suggested he wasn't pleased. "Though it was foolish to take the infection into its field of action. Is that slug alive?"

"Yes," Jai told him, checking to be sure. "Your warriors are skilled with their aim. If you had not wanted him alive – I would have left him pegged out for his creatures to feast on – let him die in the agony that he intended for your tribe."

Stacion gave his snarling grin. "I may yet." He decided. Jai heard the echo of his thought to Con. He wanted his apprentice to capture some of the snakes alive.

Jai shivered but Stacion didn't see it. What her sire could do with the evil creatures, she didn't want to think about. Setting them on their creator was one thing – using them on anyone else was obscene. Yet she could imagine Stacion enjoying the agony of his perceived enemies.

"Back to the village, woman," Stacion ordered her without acknowledging that she had done well.

Jai wasn't expecting thanks and was only too pleased to go. The warriors did not follow her. Stacion had gestured for them to stay.

Jai felt her body obeying Stacion's command at a faster pace than she wanted to run. She had to be careful not to step on any of the snakes. Con hadn't come this way with his flaming sweep. Still, Jai knew she could counter Stacion's command – once she was out of his sight.

With so much wild energy around, she could use it to sweep anything alive out of her way. A much safer option than blocking Stacion's mind, for she sensed that he was still aware of her – perhaps hoping she would step on a snake.

Jai believed that Larcia would protect her, but also that the ancient one would prefer that she learn to protect herself. So, it would be better not to experience the snake bite.

At the river, Jai came across a band of snakes trying to move from her sweep, but unwilling to enter the water. Jai leapt over them and landed in the river. With Stacion's snarl in her mind, she felt his coercion vanish. She risked a small magic to make the snakes try to follow her. Looking over her shoulder, she saw the creatures slither into the water and begin to disintegrate into steam.

Jai did not assume that all the snakes had dropped across the river, so as she trotted on at her preferred pace, her eyes scanned the ground. She was startled when she walked into something soft but solid. Instantly, she sprang back and reached for her knife.

Her eyes scanned the stranger – Kumatan – and as she began to back away, she realised that she knew him. He had the same eyes, the same face structure as her friend, Suzi. He looked like the Traeger she had outwitted.

"What do you want? This is Atapi land." Jai challenged.

"I…You're not who I expected," the young Kumatan told her.

"Fortunate for you," Jai snapped. "Stacion Ansuni eats Kumatan whelps like you for breakfast. Especially when they are spiced with Traeger training."

"He is too busy trying to control all his wild energy to notice me," the young Kumatan claimed confidently. "This exercise proves he really does need to be destroyed."

"You had better hope he stays busy and doesn't check on me again. He didn't cause this – that was the work of a would-be Stacion Ansuni. One who decided to create a cloud burst of deadly vipers – to wipe out my whole tribe."

The Kumatan waived that aside. "Then it proves that Atapi sorcery should be outlawed and its perpetrators made impotent."

"Can you honestly say that all Atapi should die?" Jai snarled.

"I didn't say that…"

"Without the sorcerers," Jai said. "The Atapi would die. Do you hate all Atapi?"

The Kumatan sighed. "No. Personally I would settle to remove the likes of Stacion Ansuni. And that other you mentioned. Do you realise that he warped the aura so much that the southern lands are being deluged by rain?"

"No – I didn't know. But it makes sense. It explains why a simple healing spell had such a strong. effect," Jai spoke more to herself.

"Healing? Is that why you are out here alone?"

"More or less. What's your name?"

The young Kumatan male looked surprised. "Jenha Mosellan – why?"

"You look like your sister," Jai said, omitting the likeness to his father. She didn't want to think about him.

"Ah! That's why you are not scared of me. Are you Jai or Bernea?"

"Jai, but I am scared for you. You should go."

"Not yet! You look like…"

"Myself!" Jai snapped. "So what are you doing here? Should I summon Stacion?"

"I am here trying to figure out how to bring the aura back to normal – you mentioned a healing spell? Can you teach it to me?"

"There are no secret words in the ritual – it is more a matter of finding what is wrong and thinking it right. I had barely started when I felt the forces eddying away from the sorcerer."

"So why were you doing it - alone? Why not Stacion Ansuni? I though all Atapi women were protected. You never seem to go anywhere without warriors."

"Curious aren't you! If you Kumatan would leave us alone we wouldn't need to! As it happens – I was sent by Stacion because I, being a healer, could sense the centre of the wrongness. He couldn't. Besides, I was merely a distraction. A female. Not dangerous. That sorcerer did not expect the warriors to spear him. Stacion wanted him alive."

"Not dangerous? My father wouldn't agree with that." Jenha countered.

"I'm nothing wonderful. Just the most dispensable healer in the tribe – no loss if I died."

Jenha seemed about to disagree, but said instead, "How did Stacion counter the snakes?"

Jai shrugged. "Con flamed some. Some drowned in the river. Stacion wants some caught."

"Why?"

"Figure it out!" Jai suggested. "They are deadly, highly poisonous and small."

"How come they left you alone?"

"I put up a healer's shield. It kept the things away until Con flamed the area."

"Con Ansuni?" Jenha queried, trying to confirm an idea. "You are friends with Stacion's whelp?"

Jai shook her head to negate that idea. "He is not like his sire."

"No. I think ... I met him," Jenha was thoughtful. "We sparred – and exchanged opinions. I think it was he I was expecting to find here – not you. Does he heal too?"

"No…"

Jai stopped talking suddenly. She felt Stacion trying to reach her mind.

Jenha's eyes widened in surprise as he sensed what Jai was doing. He stayed silent while Jai had her concentration elsewhere. Jai focussed back on him.

"You were protecting me?" Jenha asked.

"Don't think I care that much," Jai snapped. "Go before he comes here to get the snakes he thinks I am killing – and kills us both."

"You aren't scared of me?"

"Fool! Look – I like Suzi. You are not my enemy – I hope. But go! Or Stacion will kill me for talking to you. Here…"

Jai took two of her polished stones out of her belt pouch. "One for you – one for her."

"They reek of Atapi magic," Jenha almost dropped them.

"It's healing magic," Jai lied.

"If I took this into the palace – the guards will be all over it."

"Then keep them in the garden where the aura will hide them. Go!"

Jai watched Jenha walk forward and vanish. She risked the same ritual to get to a place closer to the village – near a small side trickle of water. She crouched to cup water in her hand to drink.

A force, unexpected in its power, picked her up and slammed her to the ground.

Chapter 16

Jai rolled onto her back and stared into the blazing eyes of Stacion Ansuni.

"I told you to go back, woman! Not stop and kill snakes. Jai made no attempt to defend her perceived actions.

"Where are the carcasses?"

"I flicked them into the water and they turned into steam."

Stacion kicked her, frustrated by something. "I want – some of those creatures. How can I hope to counter them if I cannot study them?"

"Majestic one – they are unnatural creatures – the touch of fire or water destroys them." Jai didn't believe his plausible explanation.

Stacion reached down and picked her up by the neck. "Do not – try – to teach me – basic sorcery."

Jai knew better than to struggle and hung limply in his grasp. "Do you have a cure for their bite? Do you know how the poison works?"

Jai had to admit that she didn't. Stacion began to walk – still holding her. Jai felt the sensation of crossing planes. When they left the blackness, Jai realised that she was back beside the river. Then she was dropped forcefully, ending up sprawled on the ground. Stacion stood over her.

"So – woman – since you think you know some basic sorcery – you will realise that once the aura goes back to normal – those creatures will die."

Jai fervently hoped so.

"Unfortunately, some fell on the village. Some were stepped on and after they had bitten the foot that squashed them – they turned to smoke. But the poison didn't. Therefore, you will seek out where the aura is still warped, and hope some of the creatures exist there. I will contain them, and you will learn from them."

Jai dared not object. Con glanced her way with concern, but she ignored him.

"My apprentice will help you."

Jai glanced then at Con, who was watching over the mangled looking body of the sorcerer. She risked touching his mind but it was solidly blocked. That told her enough. While she had been gone, Stacion had made him do things that sickened him.

Jai got to her feet as soon as Stacion strode away. She walked over to the body on the ground and realised that the sorcerer was still alive. She didn't feel sorry for him at all.

"Come, woman. We should look further up the river," Con commanded and he strode off, expecting Jai to follow. Once they left Stacion and the warriors behind, Con's manner became less rigid.

Jai still sensed that her brother was angry. He hadn't eased the block on his mind, but he spoke.

"He was going to put a shield over the village," Con stated as he stalked ahead.

Jai changed the shielding on hers to show her trudging a few paces behind Con.

"He didn't! He dragged power from me…If your healer's shield was effective – why wasn't his? Where did the power go?"

"Are you sure he wasn't lying about those in the village?" Jai asked.

"No, Bernea told me the same thing."

Jai realised that the bond between Bernea and her brother must be getting stronger – even if they had not yet mated. She hoped Stacion didn't notice. "I guess he did something to one of his enemies. When he came after me, he was more smug than angry. And if it was against the Kumatan, they can't have discovered it yet."

"What makes you say that?"

"Do you know a young Kumatan Traeger?" Jai asked.

Con nodded.

"I think he sensed me and thought it was you. Suzi's brother, Jenha Mosellan. They were aware of the warped aura and blame Stacion. He seemed decent enough for a Kumatan. I think, though that he has listened to too many of his elders. They seem to think that all sorcerers should be depowered."

"If their Traegers would leave us alone," Con growled. "The other sorcerer's would leave him alone – they've been attacking all the tribes because of him."

"Perhaps they will – if he's dead." Jai considered. "But if he's kept busy defending himself – surely his power level will be low?"

Con snorted. "Not when he draws that raw warped power into himself and sends it --- where I don't know. Yet."

"Storing it?" Jai suggested.

"Probably," Con agreed. "But for what?"

"He will be invulnerable," Jai said. "We'd need to block him from it. I was trying to find out if he was storing it in relics."

"Not from this distance," Con told her. "Anyway – can you sense any pockets of strongly warped power? I know I didn't sweep this way."

Jai concentrated. "Those snakes didn't want to go into the water. It destroys them. But they might have fled into the rocky gullies where the little creeks feed into the river after a rain. If we treat this aura like foul air – it could be trapped there."

"I don't like this – but we do need to know how the poison works." Con said.

"He said that he will make me learn," Jai said with a shudder. "I will trust Larcia and hope I won't die."

Con fed a steady stream of curses and comments through his mind as he waited for Jai to return. Now was not a good time for her to go off by crossing planes. Stacion was only too likely to arrive unexpectedly if further torturing of that sorcerer bored him. Jai hadn't told him what she was doing and he understood her silence, but did she have to do it now? He had found a squirming bunch of the poison snakes and he would have to call Stacion soon.

"I'm back," Jai spoke quietly as she returned behind him. Wordlessly, she handed him a piece of rock and one of her polished stones. He gave her a questioning look, but obeyed her gesture to put the items in his pouch.

"For the future," Jai said, opening her mind up to allow the distaste of seeing the snakes to fill her mind.

In moments, Stacion was beside her. His face was full of a horrible sort of glee.

"Go back and bring a clay pot," Con was directed.

Jai tried to shrink away from Stacion, but he grabbed her arm.

"Trying to avoid your duty to the tribe, woman?" he snarled at her. Jai shook her head.

"Good! Should you survive this and heal those at the village – you can have what is left of Ashlax for your own enjoyment."

Jai didn't react. If Stacion also knew the wight's name, he'd been bettered twice. And she had seen the condition he was in. That sorcerer would be little better than a moron – at best a puppet of Stacion's. Neither idea was appealing.

"What? Do you not like the idea of such a reward?"

Jai remained silent.

"He could be a servant," Stacion proposed. His mind sent hers a picture of an abject slave – chained to a post and only allowed to move within a limited circle. "Or you could use his body for any purpose you like."

This time he pictured her mating with the wight.

"He isn't worth the energy to heal," Jai said with deliberate scorn. "And I would not like to pollute your tribe's blood with his poison."

"But he would still be able to sire whelps – who might be sorcerers," Stacion suggested.

Jai carefully damped down her disgust. Stacion would probably kill any whelp of hers as soon as it broke shell, just to hurt her further.

To appease her sire – who was beginning to feel angry – she spoke in a tone as malicious as his, "If he lives, without my healing, and you'd wish a whelp of mixed blood – I will do as you say."

Stacion gave a grimace of pleased satisfaction. Jai hoped Con would kill him before then.

Jai writhed in agony. The bites from the snakes as she obeyed Stacion's command to pick them up and put them in the clay pot sent the pain along all of her nerve paths. Her hand felt like it was being bitten and burned and flayed – all at once.

The poison reached her blood and raced around her body and into her head which began to feel as if it would explode. The last tiny shred of logical thought directed her to draw on the aura and her fingers dug into the soil and clung. She heard in her mind the whisper of Larcia's voice.

"It is the essence of evil. It is the blood of the demons of the darkest pits of hell. Fire destroys it. Running water destroys it. A strong will can defeat it. It will destroy the pure of heart."

Jai forced her mind to think, "Thank the aura that I am not that pure of heart. I intend to kill Stacion. I claim the right – beyond life – beyond death. I claim it!"

She felt her contact with Larcia break as her fingers were dragged from the soil. She fought until she realised that Con was carrying her and feeding her his energy. It was enough for her to stay aware enough to cling to her desire for Stacion's death.

"Old Mothers," Con greeted the healers. "Stacion says that this woman holds the answers for healing those affected by the poison snakes."

He lowered Jai gently to the ground, with in the circle of healers. He sent a surge of energy to her and then left.

"Jai! Jai! It's Bernea. What must we do? Oh, she can't hear me. She's cold. Almost as cold as the spring river."

Jai reached for her friend and tried to speak, but her mind was fuzzy.

"Give her a sip of water," one of the old healers directed.

Jai sipped gratefully. It helped her mind to focus.

"Raise body temperature – in the river." Jai said, though it wasn't what she had intended to say. "Make fever," she tried again. "Running water."

"Yes!" several healers said in unison. One continued. "A fever is the body's way of fighting infection and running water is pure."

"None of our patients have a fever," another pointed out.

"So they are not fighting the poison," a suggestion was spoken. "Can we make a very high fever?"

"It's dangerous."

"Yes – but so is this poison. It is slowly and painfully killing our patients. Running water is strong with the aura. It can cool the body."

"You have to try it," Bernea insisted. "He caused this in Jai. She agreed – for the sake of the other patients."

"Jai serves the tribe well," Bernea was assured by the eldest mother. "Let her lie here for now – in the sacred circle. Even now, she draws on the aura. The others are in worse condition. We must help them first. Siluci is worst and she is a young mother with a whelp still needing her." Bernea nodded. Stacion had shown no concern for his mate – the mother of his latest child.

Stacion stared down at Jai as she lay in the women's circle. He could feel the aura surrounding her and growled. His whelp had been right. These women, the healers had some power that he had been unaware of. He would have to determine how he could control it – but not now. He needed to drain off the last of the raw power he had controlled into his hidden relics. Then he would relax and consider the chaos he had caused far away in the Kumatan city. Too far away for them to blame him. With enough power he could travel to the alien world Lancho's trader friends spoke of.

The idea intrigued him. He stalked away to his relic cave and considered what he could do on a world with no Kumatan – no Traegers. He must press Lancho for more details. His experiment today had proved instructional.

Jai couldn't move – yet her mind floated in a place that was neither the real world nor the darkness between planes.

"Child?" Larcia's mind voice sounded close.

"Am I dead?"

"No child," Larcia assured her. "Nor will you die. The aura protects you. In time it will purify the poison within you. The others will recover – thanks to your suggestions to the healers. You could heal faster if you chose."

Jai's mind considered the idea, but it was like chasing a wisp of smoke in a dense fog. She didn't like the fuzziness of her mind. "Yes, I choose."

She sensed Larcia's approval. That was enough for now.

Patiently, Jai followed Larcia's instructions for focussing her mind and calling on the aura. When her mind forgot what it was doing, Larcia gently reminded her. They would start again. After unmeasured hours, Jai's mind began to clear.

Her body, she now realised was floating in cool water, her head kept above it in a ring of bound logs. She tried to turn her head, but could not. Her eyes, when she blinked them open, showed the sky through the branches of the river trees. She tried to call out, but her voice was only a whisper that did not carry over the burble of the stream. After a time, she saw a face lean over her.

"You are awake," Bernea said with relief. She offered Jai a drink with a reed straw.

"How are the others?" Jai asked.

"Mixed," Bernea told her. "We lost two of the young children and one old warrior. The rest seem to be improving slowly. Their eyes are becoming brighter. And you?"

"Weak. But I have learnt to draw on the aura to help me. Has he come to check on me?"

Bernea snickered. "Not that one. I think he hates being near illness. He hasn't even come to check on his mate. Con has – to check on the injured warriors – of course."

"If all those here in the river are still alive – they are all warriors," Jai said. Bernea nodded agreement.

"I have things I must do," Jai said quietly.

"Are you strong enough," Bernea asked.

"I will have to be," Jai forced herself to say. "While he thinks me ill, his spies won't be watching me. And he won't sense what I am doing if he tries to read my mind."

Bernea nodded but did not ask for details. "And should he come – to check on his people – I will say you are – unfortunately – made thoroughly sick by being in running water and are indisposed in the trees yonder. There are others like that."

Jai gave a faint grin. "Help me out of this trap – will you?"

After donning dry clothing and eating a bowl of broth provided by the elder women, Jai walked to a secluded place near the village and stepped into her cave. From its hidden entrance, she observed the village. It was quiet, but it was an illusion of normality.

The women she saw all wore knives in belt sheathes. The children stayed close to their caves. The warriors walked around, always looking in all directions – expecting attack.

Of Stacion and Con, there was no sign.

Jai turned and collected her pouch of polished stones and her precious metal ingot and a small stash of food. With them, she slipped back out of the cave and quickly into cover. She sensed for a moment a mind touch. Not Stacion. He would only sense her feeling really ill at the river. Con then? She didn't react or try to reach him.

Wasting no further time, she 'walked' to the land of Loschak and on arrival, immediately felt more alive and stronger.

She looked around, opened all her senses and revelled in the complete absence of other Atapi.

A sense of urgency sent her trotting along the path to the cave behind the waterfall. She touched the bones of Loschak – this time as a gesture of respect. Her mind was full of the need to make a box like his – to inscribe all her knowledge from Larcia on it.

And if the essence of Loschak still clung to his bones, the knowledge came into her mind. The tools were still where Loschak had hidden them – in a hole behind the altar. With them were relics – power still stored in them. Once she knew what they were, she left them alone, not wanting to accidentally trigger the release of the stored power. That would be sure to draw attention to this place – both Atapi and Kumatan. She wanted neither.

Working as quickly as she could, allowing for her current weakness, Jai made a small fire in a fireplace in the cave, using charcoal, not wood. Over it she placed the clay pot with her metal ingot. Then the memories of the dead sorcerer sent her hunting for things she could see in her mind – but not identify.

The pile of objects grew - hammers for pounding, gloves of some kind of plant matter that would fit her hands, a wooden box, singed on the outside, and a number of smooth flat pieces of wood, each with a raised edge.

The wooden box was so finely crafted that none of her tribe's artificers could have matched it. Finally there was a long narrow rod of metal with a tip that scintillated in the fire's glow.

Following mental promptings and a sense of urgency, Jai worked a small ritual to make the metal liquefy without a hotter fire. She placed the flat wooden pieces on the altar and covered her hands with the gloves so she could lift the bowl of metal across to the altar. There she carefully poured the liquid metal onto the six boards so that it did not overflow the edges. She took the small excess, still in the pot, back to the fire.

Her mind supplied a ritual chant for drawing heat out of an object and with her fingers tentatively touching the wood holding the metal, she incanted it with each in turn. As she did, she felt energy coming into her. It surprised her, but some part of her mind told her that this was an ability of sorcerers and that she could use this power.

When the metal was cool to the touch of her questing finger, she turned the boards over and let the metal that had shrunken slightly, fall gently onto the altar.

She knew then, to bring the wooden box and fit the metal pieces to the sides of the same size. She realised the sense of how to assemble the box.

She brought the still hot metal back to the altar and used the metal rod, dipped into the molten metal to join the other pieces of metal together, encasing the wooden box.

It was rough compared to the exquisite box inside, but it wasn't yet finished. She used the small hammers and another ritual to soften the metal, to gently hammer out the rough edges of the join. Her mind showed her the old sorcerer's box and slowly, hers began to look like it. When she would have removed the wooden box, a sense of "NO" raced through her mind.

She tensed, feeling a threat, but then realised that it was not so much a threat as an intense desire.

Aloud, she said, "You think the wood should stay?"

Images filled her mind. The sense of them was obscure, but she guessed that some of the essence of Loschak lingered there and the long dead sorcerer somehow knew why she wanted the box.

Jai shook her head at the idea. How could a dead sorcerer know her reasons when she herself didn't completely know? But the dead one was not her enemy – his essence would be welcome.

So, she poured the rest of the metal into the wooden box, closed the lid and turned the box around and around, so that the metal coated the inside. A small ritual, she muttered then was to tell the metal how she wanted it to be. When she looked inside it was exactly as she had envisioned it.

The last of her energy seemed to flee from her and she had to sit down or fall down. It was so unexpected but she still had to do more. She drew more energy from the aura, enough to put out the fire and hide all the things she had used, except the box. She put her pot in with the other things. The metal box went into her pouch. And she took out two of her stones.

She held the stones in her hand as she walked back out through the waterfall. Back in the sunlight, she looked around and found a niche in a cairn of rocks nearby. She placed one stone there. Con, would be able to use that stone to get back here even though he had never seen the place. He had another of her stones and a piece of rock from here.

Jai felt the urgency to return and "walked" across planes to the stand of trees Bernea had indicated. She stumbled out of their seclusion and collapsed onto the ground. An old woman came over and offered her a drink.

"Hush," the woman said quietly and Jai listened and caught the sound of Stacion's ranting. The woman stayed with her until the angry tones stopped.

"He wishes his warriors back at once yet we tell him that even if the poison is gone it will take time to regain strength. He has told them that if they are not back in another day he has no use for them."

Jai shivered. "He will kill them."

The woman nodded.

"How well are they?" Jai asked urgently. "Just weak. They need food and rest. Can you think of a way for them to get it?"

Jai said nothing, but the woman read "yes" in the look they shared.

"The warriors – how is their will?"

The woman understood. "Two do not wish to weaken the tribe – the rest wish to fight."

"Which two?" Jai asked.

The woman spoke two names. "They are the oldest two – very loyal to our sorcerer."

Jai was left alone then, and she tried to draw energy from the aura – but it was not as easy here as it was on Loschak's land. She opened her senses wider and felt the aura moving away from her. She closed her senses and swore silently. "Bastard. He is taking the power we need to heal, away from the land."

<h1 style="text-align:center">Chapter 17</h1>

Con stood waiting for the women to assemble food for Stacion and his guest. The women speculated on the identity of the robed and hooded visitor, but Con was not about to reveal the truth. He stood aloof, as if being a servant was beneath him. In fact, apart from a general awareness of the women's gossip he was still listening to Stacion's conversation with Lancho – a Lancho bound in the form of the Kumatan and calling himself Lammond.

If Stacion had even suspected that Con could over hear this talk, he would have sent Con very far away, or have him unconscious. What he was over hearing was fascinating but the implications were frightening. No – terrifying.

Lancho was reporting on Stacion's meddling with a Kumatan city. The sheer devastation of the earthquake – the loss of lives, was bad enough, but that Stacion could cause it – and no Kumatan knew it – it was obscene.

But the "private" conversation had moved on and what he heard now sent his hackles erect.

Other worlds – like his own – with no Kumatan to balance the Atapi. A world with no magic to counter Stacion's. The people would be all his to play with. No! It must not be.

The girl brought the carry sack to him and bowed. Con took it, without thanks for his mind was in turmoil.

He had delayed as long as he dared. Let Stacion rant at him for being slow – he would assume that his apprentice was not interested in Lancho's report. And, he was certain that the conversation would change as soon as he returned.

He walked slowly, aware that he had missed something when the girl had brought the food. Which world did Lancho have to get a relic from? Which one of the thousands Lancho claimed to exist? Could he get Lancho to boast about it to his stupid little brother? Con began to trot faster. The conversation would be interrupted, but perhaps it would buy him time to learn.

He would have to get Jai to talk to her Kumatan friend. To find out how much of what Lancho claimed was true. It sounded improbable and perhaps it was only Lancho out to impress his sire.

Con accepted Stacion's rebuke for taking so long and Lancho's superior smirk, without comment and served the food.

As he ate his own portion, the silence was almost worse than the conversation. Lancho basked in Stacion's approval, but Stacion's thoughts were revealing.

He hadn't caused the earthquake, but he had known of it and acted to make it worse. So his power wasn't supreme – but if only he had used it to lessen the quake – he could have gained the gratitude of the Kumatan and not further enmity.

The quake, though, was probably the reason that the Kumatan had ceased harrying the tribe's borders. The fate of Stacion's prisoner had probably given the other sorcerers pause for a time.

Con stayed in Stacion's cave when Stacion 'walked' Lancho back to the northern Kumatan city. He didn't bother to look around – Stacion wouldn't be long. Instead, he risked reaching out to Jai.

"The stone?" he sent.

"Your place. Another stone is there," Jai replied tersely. "The rock is from there too. I need to talk to you – soon."

Con sent back an image of him shrugging.

Stacion returned full of satisfied arrogance.

"Those Kumatan are fools. They see only what they expect to see. Lancho hears so much because they see only an ignorant trader. When will you prove to be as useful?"

"I cannot change shape yet. I understand it is a skill of an older apprentice," Con said, which deep in his mind was equal to, "When you teach me, you bastard." He would not reveal that Jai had taught him already.

"Never mind. You are obedient and do not stint your energies," Stacion praised, and Con wondered what horrid thing he was in store for now.

"How is my mate," Stacion demanded then.

"She has survived the poison and the women are feeding her the finest food to bring her strength back quickly."

Con thought he heard his sire mutter something like "weakling".

"Select me two, young, well fleshed women," Stacion ordered.

Con merely nodded. He knew of a couple who would not object to Stacion's attentions, were attractive enough, but who would quickly lose Stacion's interest. Once his sire was occupied Con hoped to have time for himself.

It wasn't to be. Stacion gave him a list of things to do before morning. The first of them was to make the prisoner eat and drink.

Jai waited for Con to contact her but when night fell, she knew she could wait no longer. In the darkness, she slipped to where the younger warriors lay, still trying to regain their strength.

"Quiet. Listen." She said when one challenged her. "Will you be well enough to return to your duties tomorrow?"

"We must," one stated. "Or we will no longer be warriors."

"If you aren't?" Jai probed.

Each of the five said nothing.

"You are torn," Jai told them. "So, if you must choose between the good of the tribe and dying because of the heartless order of one intent on his own whims – what would you choose?"

"To live. To fight," they hissed quietly. Two of the warriors glanced to one side where the two old warriors were sleeping.

"Can you not heal us faster?"

"No. The aura is being drained from here," Jai said, pausing to let them draw their own conclusions. "I could take you – elsewhere."

"You?" one queried.

"Yes!" the others agreed over the doubt of the first.

"Tomorrow," Jai promised. "Be ready."

She slipped away. Her next move was the dangerous one.

Chapter 18

Jai prepared her mind shield to seem like one in an exhausted but restless sleep. Then she let her mind seek for the stone she had given the young Kumatan – Jenha. She hoped he had given it to his sister as she had asked. Her own essence was on that stone. If that Kumatan knew how, he could find her using it. It was a risk, but she believed that Jenha was not like his sire yet.

With the stone pictured in her mind, she sensed the aura around it. The sense of Kumatan came first. She had expected that. She could not tell if the stone was near any of them. It would not be wise, anyway, to appear in her own form. She recalled how she had changed into Kumatan form as a response to danger. Now she wanted to change to be ready for it.

Her body remembered it, that other shape, and flowed into it. She felt as she had in the river – gently massaged.

Then she 'walked' forward three steps. On the third step, as she arrived, she quickly took a step backwards.

The figure she had walked into spun around, and Jai tensed for action.

"You keep walking into me," Jenha Mosellan chided softly. He had recognised her at once.

Jai relaxed a bit. "I hoped to see Suzi," she said, feigning calm.

"I have called her," Jenha said after a moment. "What brings you here? Are you a spy?"

"No. I came to ask a favour of you."

"Of me?"

"Yes. But I don't know if it would be against your – ethics."

"My father would say that the Atapi know nothing of ethics."

Jai shook her head. "Do you always obey your father? Agree with him?"

"I am meant to – is the first answer and 'no' for the second."

"Then we have much in common," Jai pointed out. "I need your help."

"Why would you trust me to help you?"

A female voice answered before Jai could. "Because Jai and I are friends and even you agree that Atapi and Kumatan don't have to be enemies."

"Some Atapi," Jai corrected, tensing slightly as Suzi embraced her.

A loud clamour of bells broke the silence and Jai shivered in fear. Then she sensed Con and her instinct screamed, "Con – change!"

A young looking, big eyed, Kumatan stumbled into the clear area. He stared warily at Jenha, who was returning the regard. Suzi seemed to know at once who it was and grabbed him as she had Jai.

Jenha reached for Jai and directed her face to his and forced their heads together. Suzi copied his actions with Con.

"Guards are coming, relax," Jenha whispered.

Jai found it wasn't easy to relax, but she realised that if Jenha was going to reveal them as enemies he would have done so as soon as she had arrived.

Con, in an unfamiliar body and entangled with Suzi, was fighting the instinct to defend himself as the guards appeared with weapons raised.

The weapons were lowered when the guards recognised Jenha.

"My lord Mosellan, what are you doing?"

Suzi answered with a pout. "It should be obvious. It is the first chance we have had since being gaoled here to see our friends."

"My lady, this is not a gaol. And it is highly inappropriate behaviour. Especially when your father is away on important business."

"Don't be a snob," Suzi pouted again. "I like Conanta. He is a lot more fun that all those arrogant snobs that father thinks I should like."

"And you my lord?"

Jenha simply held Jai and said nothing.

After a moment, the guard leader sighed. "Well, keep away from the intruder barrier."

Jenha nodded and he watched the squad leave.

"Will there be trouble?" Jai asked. "Will they wonder how we got here?"

Jenha released her and Suzi let Con free.

"No, they will assume you snuck in with the traders and we brought you here," Suzi said with a laugh. "They will believe that of me. Father will be annoyed, though not as much as Suni when she hears. But then, she's a bitch anyway. I like her twin, Ellhi, better."

Jai looked lost. Suzi quickly explained, "Suni thinks Jenha is hers."

"Traders," Con interrupted. "Are they here? Can I see them?"

"Con!" Jai broke in. "Not now – we have got to do something else first."

Con glanced at Jai and saw her intense expression. "What?"

Jai in turn glanced at Jenha and Suzi and chose her words carefully. She explained things to Con, but only what she wanted the Kumatan to hear.

Con controlled his anger and said, "You have a plan?"

Jai nodded. "I promised the five younger warriors the chance to fight. I know a place where they won't be found by any sorcerers and they won't bother the Kumatan and where the aura is strong and they can recover. As they cannot with Stacion stealing the aura they need."

"What would you need of me?" Jenha asked.

Jai outlined her plan. Con grinned his approval.

"I don't see that I have a problem here – except for killing two weak warriors," Jenha agreed.

Con considered. "They will not recover by Stacion's deadline. No doubt he will make me kill them anyway. If you do not wish to – I will. You can simply provide the traces of an ambush – we can do the rest."

"What if this ambush stirs your sorcerer to move against us?" Jenha asked.

"And he isn't already," Jai muttered. "If you aren't already stirring him up with your vendetta?"

"Stacion is not expecting trouble from you – not with the destruction of your northern city. And not from the other sorcerers since he reduced one bright young sorcerer to witless slave. A sneak attack – with no warning..." Con suggested.

"It is an excellent opportunity. Father won't fault me. He need not have the full details. It will aid your plot against him?"

Con nodded. "I must do what I can to save the tribe from him. And if you and your kind continue as you have been, I can remove one or two people to a safer place each time."

"And if women disappear while foraging," Jai added. "He will blame the encroaching sorcerers."

"Won't he go after them?" Jenha asked. He then answered his own question. "No, perhaps not. Father has one of his warriors as a prisoner, and your sorcerer has never tried to free him. My father would never leave one of his men in Atapi hands."

Con stared at Jenha as he spoke of the prisoner. He then shared a look with Jai.

"When do you want me?" Jenha asked.

Jai mentioned a time and place – just before dawn.

"Are you strong enough," Suzi demanded.

"What's wrong" Jai asked.

"Some snake thing bit him," Suzi told them. "He has only just got out of bed."

"How did you survive?" Jai asked.

"The healers recognized Atapi poison and knew what to do," Suzi claimed.

"And I held tight to your healing stone," Jenha added.

"No. It was your will that kept you alive – as mine did." Jai told him.

"Were you bitten too? Are you better?" Suzi asked.

"Still weak," Jai admitted. "But it is odd that I feel better here in the place of perceived enemies than I do at home."

"Did the stone heal me?" Jenha asked.

"Perhaps," Jai considered. "Though it is probably acting as a conduit for you from the aura. If you are not able to draw on it yourself."

"I'd like to know more about that ability," Jenha hinted.

Con interrupted. "Not now. That and traders must wait. Jai – we have to go."

Con left first. He changed back to his true form before departing. Jai left moments later, returning to the river.

Chapter 19

While Jai took half of the women from the river to the new land – both patients and healers, Con was summoned back to Stacion to report on the duties he had been set. Stacion had dismissed the women but his lair smelt of mating and blood.

"Did our prisoner eat?" Stacion demanded. He was dressing in a formal robe that allowed his wings to be free.

"Yes, Master. He had no choice."

"Good. I do not want him to starve to death. I promised him to your freak womb mate. I will insist that she uses him as a mate. I will go and place a compulsion on him to obey her."

"You would introduce such vile blood into your tribe," Con asked.

"No, but a child of that blood would be valuable as a bargaining piece. That tribe would pay dearly for it, especially when its sire is dead."

"It would also have blood from this tribe," Con argued.

"It will not be a child of this tribe," Stacion roared. "And none of mine admitted to siring that female."

Con stared back stoically, but thinking in a shielded part of his mind that his sire was a hypocrite.

"Then I suppose that I should not begrudge that monster his food," Con spoke callously, knowing that Stacion would approve. "However, I am not sure that creature really is as cowed as he acts. His eyes show cunning."

Stacion reacted as Con hoped he would. "I have his name! He is mine. His will is mine."

Con refrained from asking, "Are you sure?"

Instead he asked, "Did he tell you his name? Did he scream it at you or whisper it?"

"He screamed," Stacion answered as if savouring a memory. "Why?"

"Only that should I get a secret name – I would not want to share it. If forced to reveal it – I'd whisper and hope they couldn't hear it properly."

Stacion gave his snarling grin. "He spoke truly."

Con shrugged. "Are you going somewhere?"

"To the Rock of Arkor. I have demanded a meeting of all the tribal sorcerers. I will warn them of the consequences of continuing to harry my lands. You will remain here."

Con was relieved. "Of course, Master." While he really wanted to know what happened at the meeting, he needed to help work Jai's plan. And that would go better with Stacion out of the way.

It seemed that when Stacion finally appeared to survey the scene, that most of the damage had been cleared away.

"Kumatan," Stacion snarled since their aura had been made deliberately strong. "Cowards! Attacking old warriors and children."

Con looked up from his task of laying out the two old warriors. They had taken their own lives, but he had made it look as if others had.

The women were dragging the bodies of two children and two more warriors from the stream. These had all died of the poison before the 'attack'.

"Master, your other warriors have forced off the attackers, but I fear still have not the strength to last out. And some of the women are missing – drowned I fear."

Stacion stood still a moment, then said, "The warriors are no more – I cannot sense them. Leave the bodies for carrion. They were no longer warriors."

Con was about to speak again when Stacion proclaimed, "The rest of these malingerers can recover in their caves."

Since that was what he wanted Stacion to think, Con merely nodded. "I will finish here, Master, unless there is something more urgent for me to do?"

Stacion gestured in the negative.

Con dutifully reported yet another disappearance to Stacion. The sorcerer ignored the loss of yet another female and merely flicked his mind out to seek the warrior before pronouncing the warrior dead. He had decreed that he had no wish to learn the fate of stupid females. They did him a favour.

Stacion had not stopped to total the losses or really noticed the dwindling numbers. He was too busy brooding on some plan he had conceived. Con feared that he knew what it was.

Stacion had convinced or coerced the other sorcerers to leave him alone. The Kumatan raids were like transient itches to him.

He didn't even insist on tormenting Jai – who he believed to be still weak and helpless – like his mate Siluci. He believed that since his mate was being given the best treatment, so of course Jai would be worse off as an unimportant female. He didn't seem to realise that Siluci would be relishing the attention and deliberately be prolonging being helpless. Nor did he realise that Siluci was becoming more disillusioned with her mate than seemed possible.

Con had a growing colony on his land, every one of them loyal to him and bound to protect his land. He had tried to convince Bernea to go there for safety. She refused, saying that Stacion was used to seeing her and might notice if she wasn't around. That had been a concern for him and the reason why Jai stayed with him. Of the elders and healers, many would swear to him, but chose to stay and help him with Stacion. Another that could not be spirited away was the artisan, Laguno. Stacion was aware of him since he had presented him with his newest prized possession – the jewelled knife and sheath.

Soon enough Con knew he would have to challenge Stacion, but he did not feel ready. Even with his secret trips to the Rock of Arkor, he still felt he had too much still to learn.

Jai was helping him with that – she was seeking knowledge for him as well as recording the Atapi Lore for herself. He had asked her why, but she had been unable to explain. It was not as if she would ever be denied access there by the power that mattered – Larcia.

Jai was in fact feeling fully recovered, for the aura in Arkor filled her. Yet on the odd occasions that Stacion tried to check on her, he only sensed extreme lethargy. His mind revealed a mixture of pleasure that she was helpless and annoyance that he could not yet force her to couple with his prisoner.

Jai spent as much time as she could in her dreaming place looking for Atapi lore that could help Con defeat his sire. There was so much knowledge recorded on the rock that it was taking too much time. Finally, she dared to ask Larcia for help.

"How can Con possibly win against Stacion? He has enough power to make a Kumatan city quake."

"The quake was a natural event," Larcia corrected her.

"Perhaps – but he made the damage worse than it would have been." Jai argued.

Larcia went silent. Jai had begun to believe that at those times Larcia was looking through the aura.

"You are right, daughter," Larcia said with an icy voice. "All the quake defences were negated – blasted."

"How could Con defend against that?" Jai asked.

"Small power, applied thoughtfully, can have a major effect," Larcia advised. "Read the works of Inshak and Bruschek."

Jai spent the time until the sun faded – fascinated by the two accounts written by young sorcerers who had defeated more powerful rivals.

"The older ones were complacent and arrogant," Jai said. "Like Stacion, thinking their power supreme. But I cannot see how a tiny whirlwind could kill."

"One used it as a distraction," Larcia explained. "The other used it as a finely tuned weapon. Imagine the power of a large showy whirlwind, concentrated in one the size of your hand."

Jai couldn't.

"Watch. Listen." Larcia instructed.

Jai heard in her mind the ritual and saw the small whirlwind forming in the sand of her dreaming place. It began to move, forming a furrow in the sand.

"Copy it!" Larcia ordered.

Jai studied the whirlwind and understood the forces involved. In moments, a second whirlwind twined around the first. The original one then faded into a wisp of a breeze.

"Make it move with your mind. Send it; see it where you want it to go. Send it to the rock shelf."

Jai concentrated and the tiny whirlwind moved slowly to the base of the rock, leaving a furrow behind it.

"Lift it," Larcia directed.

That was more difficult. Jai imaged the thing rising and it seemed to become larger.

"Keep it small," Larcia directed her.

She needed a different mind image and pretended the wind rested on a tiny stone and pictured the stone rising to be level with the rock shelf. Once there she kept it steady until Larcia added a new challenge.

"Look at what it is doing to the rock."

In amazement, Jai saw a hole being bored by the tiny wind.

"Now," Larcia suggested. "See if you can make it do that on the rock wall. Write something."

By the time Jai had finished, she had learnt to fully control the wind weapon and had thought of a handful of ways it could be used.

"It buzzes like a fly," Jai said. "A sorcerer would ignore a fly during a battle but he couldn't ignore a big whirlwind."

"A big one is more obvious, more awkward to control and needs more power to make it and move it," Larcia said finally. "And the more the aura is warped, the easier it is to counter as the aura will work with you to return to what is natural."

"The trouble is Con says Stacion has power relics hidden all over the tribes land. He drew in as much as he could of the warped energy that he could and siphoned it off. But that sorcerer had drawn most of it from our land…"

"Then you must find a way to block those relics from him," Larcia said. "If you know what they are, you can make his mind forget them."

"What if he senses what I am doing?"

"Has he yet?" Larcia countered.

"No, but – I've never seen his relic cave."

"Your brother has."

"Then he could block them?"

"Unwise, daughter. Stacion would be alert to meddling from a rival."

"Oh," Jai uttered. "I doubt if even Con knows them all."

"Any that you learn of – if removed could help."

"Couldn't we – trigger them and send the power back into the aura?"

"No, for they are such that they are separated from the aura – so the power does not leech away. Only their creator is attuned to them. If another should meddle – Stacion would be aware of it. It is likely that there would be a concussion of power."

Jai sighed and put the matter in the back of her mind to think on.

Jai walked slowly across the open space – pretending to still be convalescing. She had deemed it time to be seen around. Although not seeming to be paying attention to the activities of the village, she sensed the alert watchfulness of all the tribe – even the children.

No one spoke to her, but that was normal. Few would openly acknowledge her, but to briefly meet her eyes was safe enough.

When she sensed feet padding along behind her, she stopped and turned suddenly. The slave clad figure ran into her. The figure was taller than her by half a head, so even though adopting the posture of a newly made slave - he seemed to be looking down his nose at her.

"You!" Jai snarled at the sorcerer who had created the rain of snakes. "What do you want?"

"Mistress, I am sent to serve you." The tone was subservient but the gleam in his eyes was not. "Master Stacion sent me to you. I am to show you the cave he has granted you for your selfless healing of…"

"Your victims." Jai snarled again. Her sire had pictured this creature chained up, not walking around free. He still bore the scars and not fully healed wounds of the torture Stacion had inflicted, but he was by no means the broken spirit he was pretending to be.

A cave? Of her own? Jai stilled a shudder. She remembered the rash promise she had made about using this creature as a mate – if he recovered without the healers helping him. It seemed that he had but, for a defeated sorcerer whose powers would have been taken from him - who had been tortured nearly to death, he had recovered fast. Too fast.

"Where is this cave?" Jai decided to ask. She had spotted Stacion watching from a reclining place outside his cave.

"Follow me, Mistress."

He too must have noticed Stacion's regard, because now his body language was indeed that of a mind broken slave.

The cave was close to Stacion's. Too close for comfort, but Jai did not intend to leave anything there that she wanted to keep private. It was also filthy – full of blown in dust, leaves as well as the bones of dead creatures.

Jai stared at the mess. The slave was watching her from lowered eyes, but he was glancing every so often towards the opening.

"So, you are to serve me," Jai said as if musing. "Well, whatever your name is, you can sweep out this mess. Right now this cave looks like an animal pen and fit only for the likes of you."

The searing look in the ex-sorcerer's eyes quickly changed to a slave's dull eyed look.

"You heard what she said, Ashlax, do as she tells you," Stacion spoke harshly. Jai turned and bowed respectfully to her tribal leader, as the slave ran out to obey the command.

"You can do what you like to him," Stacion said as if bestowing a great favour. "I have compelled him to obey you. If he displeases you, I will have him whipped."

Stacion stalked off. Jai knew he would have her whipped if she didn't keep her rash promise.

Jai shuddered. For the first time in her life, he'd spoken – not kindly – but at least neutrally to her. He hadn't thanked her for her healing services but simply indicated that he had kept this pledge. It was the closest to 'nice' that he had ever been to her and it frightened her. Her mind burgeoned with ideas that she dare not think on. Stacion would be watching her, reading her mind, to be sure she obeyed him.

So she occupied her mind with how to set the cave to rights. What she thought she could appropriate for her use and how she would arrange things. Then she considered how to keep the damn slave secured when she had no job for it. Then she thought about going to the waste pit as if that had been her intention before being accosted.

A faint pressure left her mind. Very quickly, she warded her mind, so if Stacion checked in a while, he would think she was attending a natural function. Jai walked past the privy pit anyway, as she had not had a specific purpose, except to be seen. As she walked, she made plans. If Ashlax was truly Stacion's creature, he would be obeying Stacion as well as her. No doubt Stacion's orders would have precedence. Also, he would be a constant spy for Stacion, watching her every move.

However, she was convinced that Ashlax was acting a role and for his own reasons. If so this was so, then she needed to know what he intended to do and why. She was sure of one thing; he had no friendly feelings towards Stacion Ansuni.

The vileness of his attack and his disregard for innocent Atapi was at odds with his manner now. If he still threatened her tribe, Jai wanted to know. But how to find out?

A cloud of dust was emerging from the cave as she approached from one side. As soon as she was fully in the opening, the amount of dust was reduced. Jai had time to notice the broom whisking vigorously by itself before Ashlax grabbed it. She pretended she had noticed nothing odd. It did however, confirm her instinct. The sorcerer wasn't broken; he could still use his power. Jai flicked a warning to Con before removing the warding on her mind.

"Slaves usually do not work so fast," Jai said with a hint of warning in her tone. She glimpsed a flash of fear, quickly quelled. He would assume her to be a favourite of Stacion, and think she might betray his lapse to him. She wondered if he could be used as an ally against Stacion Ansuni.

"I wished to be efficient for the Mistress," Ashlax bowed with the appropriate deference.

"You can forget the gratuitous comments Ashlax. I don't believe them and I don't like you. You will work without talking and talk only when I ask you something. Do you understand?"

"Yes, Mistress," was his reply.

"Good. When you have finished sweeping, go to the older women and ask for two canine skins for the floor and a mattress cover of hare skins. You can stuff that with soft ferns."

Jai walked out, towards the artisans conclave, moving slowly and seemingly unaware of the figure following her. Jai spoke to the weavers and asked for a piece of fabric to use as a privacy curtain and then went to Laguno.

The artificer bowed to her.

"Mistress Jai, I am in your debt. Our leader was so impressed by the knife and its sheath that he rewarded me with gold."

"You deserve it, old one," Jai smiled. "But can you give me something to hang a curtain on?"

Laguno trotted off and returned with a coil of rope, and two pointed metal pieces with rings at one end. He also brought a mallet of granite bound to a wooden handle.

Jai thanked him and walked back to her cave. She spotted Ashlax carrying a bundle and coming from the direction of the women's area. Jai reached the cave first, unsurprised that the dust was gone, even though she knew that Ashlax had left moments after her and when there had still been a lot of mess to clear.

Jai directed Ashlax to put the mattress in an alcove, the canine rugs on the floor and to hang the curtain. As an afterthought, she added for him to prepare a fire place – near the opening – and to find an eight foot long tree trunk, narrow enough for her to put two hands around.

Again, Jai walked out on him, and again he emerged from the cave. If he needed a reason, the ferns and pole would serve him.

Bernea trotted towards her. Jai slowed her pace, so she was still near enough for Ashlax to hear.

"Jai! Barisk has cut his foot. You are needed."

Jai trotted off with Bernea.

"That slave is following," Bernea whispered.

"Thought as much. He is spying on me for…" Jai shrugged in the direction of Stacion's cave.

Bernea moved away from Jai as she continued on to the women's area.

Barisk was lying in the healing circle, his head in the lap of the unmated female he was interested in. They were whispering, and oblivious to the Elder mother tending the gash.

"You stitch the gash, daughter," Jai was told. She moved aside to wash her hands in an astringent solution.

"Beware your slave," the old woman warned when she returned.

"I am," Jai agreed. "He acts the role of slave better for Stacion than he does for me."

"Indeed. Stacion is to be feared."

"Then he ought to fear me more," Jai whispered. "For I know his name – truly."

"It is not enough," the Elder Mother spoke. "There are words…"

When the woman stopped speaking, Jai glanced up and saw Stacion approaching. She waited for the Elder Mother to hold the edges of the wound together so she could begin to stitch.

"Barisk, if you do not lie still I will have Jai stitch both of your feet together," the woman said in a voice loud enough to carry. The girl talking to Barisk sobered at once.

"A fine would-be warrior you are," the girl scolded. "This is a chance to prove your courage."

Jai felt Stacion's mind flick across hers. Quicker than normal. Did he dislike the sight of injured flesh being stitched?

The old woman began to speak again when Stacion had gone. Her voice was a barely perceptible whisper.

"All the sights you've ever seen – gone

All the places you've ever been – gone

All the sounds you've ever heard – gone

Jai repeated the three lines. "Shouldn't there be more?"

"Yes, but that should be enough to frighten him. He will realise that you have enough power to enforce it."

"Wouldn't it be better to remove his power?" Jai asked.

"You must decide if he is of more use alive or dead."

"You think that he could be used?"

"Even a flawed tool can be used," the Elder advised.

Chapter 20

Ashlax was waiting in the cave when she returned. He squatted in a slave's pose by the entrance. Jai saw that everything was as she had directed. The pole lay to one side. Jai had walked past Ashlax, seeming to ignore him, but she turned suddenly to catch him as he was rising to his feet. He continued the movement, even though she was watching him.

No Atapi turned slave, would dare stand in his master or mistress's presence without permission.

"Stacion called you Ashlax. What was your tribal name?" Jai asked.

"Danderon of the tribe of Sonon," the one called Ashlax admitted.

"Well, Danderon, a word of advice. You may think you have fooled Stacion into believing he has mastered you, but I know better. If you continue to use magic to do your slave's duties he will notice."

"And who will tell him, woman!" Ashlax taunted, moving closer.

"I would take great pleasure in doing so," Jai admitted, standing her ground. "I would take pleasure in watching him torture you over and over again. I detest you. You created vile creatures that killed innocent children and women as well as warriors. Did you prepare an antidote to the poison before you created it?"

"Of course," he boasted, as he arrogantly strode forward and grabbed Jai.

"Let me go, Auslak," Jai commanded.

He obeyed, but said, "Its Ashlax."

"Larcia wither your maleness if you try to touch me like that again," Jai told him coldly. She saw a sheen of sweat forming on Ashlax's face. "What instructions did Stacion give you regarding me, Auslak?"

"To watch you and report to him. To be your servant." Ashlax spoke with obvious reluctance.

"All of it," Jai commanded.

"He said you would be grateful to have me as a plaything, and should I sire a whelp on you he would release me."

Jai nodded and with relief sensed Con entering the cave.

Ashlax did too. He spun around, recognised Con and his face turned an odd shade and the sweat increased.

"It is not me you should fear, worm," Con told him coldly.

Ashlax straightened, and gathered his courage, more like bravado. "I don't," he claimed. "Nor do I fear your master."

"No, because you think you have fooled him. You think you have succeeded in being a spy in our midst," Con commented. "You may think you will succeed in diluting or polluting our tribe with your blood, but once you succeed in creating a cross bred whelp – Stacion will have no further use for you. He will have a lever to coerce your tribe and you will be dead."

"And since I have his blessing to do what I want to with you," Jai broke in, "I will have you staked out on the ground, with those snakes Stacion captured poured over you, so you will suffer like you have made this tribe suffer."

Ashlax made a dash for the door. Con grabbed him.

"It is time you learnt who your master really is," Con said ignoring the struggles. Con nodded to Jai.

"All the sights you've ever seen – gone, Auslak,

All the places you've ever been – gone"

Jai seemed to pause at the end of the second line, so that Ashlax could break in.

"No! It cannot be you!"

"Can't it?" Jai asked gently. "Because I am only a healer? Only a female? I have your secret name. How else could I know that? You didn't tell Stacion. You were defeated my ME. Larcia whispered your name to me. I am your master now. You are no longer a sorcerer, no longer welcome at Arkor."

"Larcia is a myth," Ashlax said desperately.

"Is she? I invoked her and you felt your maleness wither."

The shudder that raked Ashlax proved that he acknowledged that fact.

"You are mine, Auslak. Swear loyalty to me, swear on Larcia's name."

Shaking and trembling, Ashlak spoke the oath, knowing that he was beaten, was nothing. Should he be forsworn, his mind would be turned to mush.

Jai eased out a relieved breath. Con nodded in approval. Ashlax studied the floor.

"Con, could you stand that pole, over near the door," Jai asked. "My servant will stay tethered to it until I feel I can trust him."

Con tensed his posture. "An intelligent thought. I would not trust this worm either."

Con began to chant a ritual and the pole began to move. Stacion arrived unannounced, though both Jai and Con had been aware of his coming.

"Are you pleased with your reward?" Stacion asked Jai without really acknowledging her.

"Majestic One, I am overwhelmed by your generosity, your recognition of my poor skills. This slave is so fearful of your displeasure that he works fast and correctly."

Stacion snarled a grin and stalked away. He hadn't missed the pole being erected and no doubt had heard that the slave was to be tethered there. She risked brushing his mind. He was convinced that Ashlax would still put his orders above those of the woman.

Con left as soon as he had finished. Jai told Ashlax to sit by the post and she sat on the bed and stared at him. She tried to touch his mind and couldn't. After a while she realised that the 'sorcerer's overmind' ability only worked with those who shared the same blood.

After trying to think of a way to overcome that problem and only coming up with the one that was distastefully obvious – it occurred to her that Stacion would not be able to read his mind either. He would have to rely on Ashlax speaking the truth. What would her slave tell him?

"Auslak, when Stacion asked you about me, what did you say?"

Compelled, Ashlax recited what he had seen. Jai was relieved. He had not been spying on her for long.

"Auslak, when he asks again, you will tell him only that I have been doing my womanly tasks," Jai listed her normal chores. "There is no need to report how many times I need to slip off to the privy – or that you follow me when I go to wash in the river. In fact you will not follow me unless I permit it."

"I will obey, mistress," Ashlax stared at his feet.

"And Auslak, should he ask if I have allowed you to mate with me – well, as a slave you dare not be too forward and I must be a sheltered virgin, ignorant of such things."

"Yes, Mistress," he agreed again.

"And in truth, the idea nauseates me. I know what you did and I have no wish to give you what you want until I have tormented you for a very long time."

Jai knew that her last words would be repeated as she hadn't forbidden him to repeat them. Knowing Stacion, he would then probably put some spell on Ashlax to make her unable to resist him. Before then, however, she would speak to the Elder Mothers to get a potion from them to make Ashlax permanently impotent.

Jai ignored her slave for the rest of the afternoon, savouring his defeat and considering how she could use him against Stacion.

Without seeming to be willing, by being forced to mate with Ashlax, the scum of Atapi maleness – Stacion would feel he'd won, but instead, she would. Intimacy with Ashlax would open his mind to hers – giving her further power over him. Power Stacion would never suspect.

Jai knew that Stacion was watching her and she amused him by tormenting her slave unmercifully. She sensed Stacion's laughter in her mind as her words cut into the former sorcerer's deflated ego.

She also learned that he had summoned the Eldest Mother and asked when it would be fortuitous for Jai to become with egg. Stacion was unaware of the tone of censure in the Eldest Mother's voice when she answered.

"With that one – her female time will be when the moon is dark for she was born at that time."

Still amused at the plight of his prisoner, Stacion waved the Eldest Mother away and decided a week or two was not too long to wait.

Jai was not surprised when she smelt benit weed in her slave's morning drink. Her own held a different herb, one that would stop her fertile cycle. The mothers were taking no chances and Jai knew they did not approve of Stacion's intentions.

Chapter 21

Jai watched with deep satisfaction as Con bound himself to the lands once belonging to Loschak. All that had belonged to Loschak was now Con's. This included a large number of power relics that had become more powerful by slow absorption of the aura over a period of two hundred years. The sixty or so Atapi now living there – approached one by one and pledged themselves to Con and the new land. In doing so, they severed ties to Stacion's land.

When it was Jai's turn, she hesitated. Though she fully supported Con, some instinct made her hesitate. "Con, you know I will support you with all that I am, but I feel that now is not the time for me to bind myself to this land. Although I have power, I am not a sorcerer. You can still have bindings to two places – I cannot. I feel I must stay bound to Stacion's land if I am to help you best."

Con accepted her reasons.

"Then, womb-mate, you had best keep all you hold dear, or need, to hand. For when the showdown comes you may need to flee with no warning."

"Yes," Jai agreed, sensing some subtle change in her brother. He seemed more confident, wiser. "I will, but I must go back – be seen."

Con nodded. Jai was right. What if Stacion sensed her change of loyalty? He might, since he was waiting for word that she was with egg.

The past three weeks had been peaceful. Stacion, with his intent interest in Jai and her slave had meant that he was not doing other acts to annoy outsiders and which required that assistance of his apprentice. Jai had less time to visit Larcia and the Rock of Arkor, but Con had more.

However, Stacion would soon tire of waiting.

Jai sensed Ashlax trudging after her and sighed. The persistent presence of her slave was beginning to irritate her. She would forbid him to follow her but Stacion had ordered him to stay close and it was wiser to tolerate it than for Stacion to suspect her own control of the slave.

Bernea joined Jai as they were both going to the women's area to help the Elder Mothers checking all the tribe's children for spotted fever.

"Well, how did it go?" Bernea asked.

"What?" Jai asked in return.

"You know – you and that slave," Bernea clarified.

Jai felt her face flush in anger, not embarrassment.

"Does everyone know that I finally debased myself to mate with that worm?" she demanded in a whisper.

"Probably," Bernea admitted. "Stacion's yes-men were arguing about whether you get with egg this cycle."

The 'yes-men' as Bernea described a group of older warriors – had long since lost the notion of independent reasoning and obeyed Stacion implicitly. They were like the two who had been affected by Ashlax's snakes who had killed themselves because Stacion has said they were no longer warriors and were therefore useless.

"So that is what was bothering Ashlax earlier," Jai muttered. "Were they saying I'd forced myself on him? Someone seemed to think I'd be desperate enough to do just that."

Bernea knew she meant Stacion Ansuni.

"Yes. They despise that slave. The idea of you raping him was highly amusing."

Jai felt the heat increase in her face.

"Well, in answer to your question. It was an experience I'd rather repeat with a male of my choosing. That slave still hasn't learnt his place. He still has a sorcerer's arrogance even if he can't use the aura any more."

Jai walked away from Bernea and went to one of the Elder Mothers and listened to what she was told to do.

Her first task was to tend to the group of children who already had the fever and spots. Once the fever had flared, these children had been unable to keep any food or liquid in them. It meant that they would not be able to retain the herbal remedy that mitigated the disease, for long enough for it to be effective. Her task was to draw on the aura to overcome that symptom, for long enough for the mixture to work.

Later she would help with the children who simply needed to drink the unpleasant tasting liquid.

To get the liquid into the sickest children, she used a bent reed that fitted into a bubble of tree gum. She had to insert the reed into the child's throat before slowly squeezing the medicine in. Sometimes, in spite of her efforts the child was immediately sick and she would have to begin again to calm them, numb their throat and call on the aura.

One of these was Siluci's whelp. Siluci was distraught and of no help in calming her son.

Jai tuned Siluci out and concentrated on the boy, called Lucion. Vaguely, she heard a gentle voice talking to Siluci, and getting her to sit and sip something. Then, when Lucion was finally calm, she felt a new reed and bulb pressed into her questing hand.

When the medicine was down, Jai concentrated on keeping Lucion calm until enough time had passed and then handed him back to his mother.

"He will be alright won't he?" Siluci asked, jumping up.

"He needs rest," Jai said quietly. "And regular drinks of the herbal solution. See the elder mothers for it."

Jai finally noticed her helper and was astonished to see Ashlax there.

"Why did the Elder Mothers let you in?" she asked, as she drew in more energy from the aura. "You are a male!"

All he answered was, "I am your slave. It is my duty to serve you."

All very proper! But his mind answer surprised her. "I wish to atone for the pain I inflicted on the tribe."

Jai heard the unspoken reason and felt his sincerity. She tensed. She didn't want to believe him. Her mind said – "I want to keep hating him."

His mind thought, "I only deserve to be hated. Oh Holy …. I heard her mind and she heard me. It isn't possible. No female can do that, not even one with my tribe's blood. Not even another sorcerer can since I received my secret name. Have I sunk that low? If a woman can read my mind – could Stacion Ansuni? What is she? Oh my! The power in her…"

Jai whispered fiercely. "Auslak – you will never, ever, mention that to anyone! I am a healer – that is all."

The force of that command settled on him. He nodded. So many ideas flittered through his mind that Jai couldn't follow them. Finally, he thought at her. "Can Stacion do this to me?"

Jai shook her head as the next of the very ill children was brought to her.

As she examined the little girl, she thought back. "I am told that the sorcerer can only use the skill of 'overmind' on those of his blood."

"I believed that also," Ashlax agreed mentally.

"However, when a sorcerer steals a woman from another tribe – he comes to be able to use the skill on her." Jai went on.

"Ah! Intimacy! Woman, you are diabolically clever."

"And you are still an arrogant bastard," Jai retorted before tuning him out and concentrating on her patient.

Ashlax seemed to stalk off, but he was soon back with another cup of warm herbal brew for the mother of the patient. He silently helped her when he could.

When Jai was once again alone, he spoke again.

"My apologies, Jai Mistress. I hated you because I believed Stacion thought highly of you – because he gave me to you."

Jai unblocked her mind and thought, "No, he simply joined the dregs of his tribe with the scum of another. He will lose nothing and possibly gain an important pawn."

"He dishonours us both," Ashlax said quietly. "Obviously he doesn't know…"

"He knows I am a healer of modest ability," Jai prevented him from thinking about her true power. He jerked and nodded, instantly understanding.

"There are undercurrents of unspoken thoughts," Ashlax said softly. "Things that make no sense to me – but I swear on Larcia's name, that I will do all in my power to help you with your intentions. If I still had the power to do magic…"

Jai thought at him, "You would have betrayed yourself and now be very dead."

"How did you know the words of the ritual to remove my power?"

"Think! Don't speak! Stacion's yes-men are still hovering to report on you."

"Can't Stacion read your mind?"

Jai smiled faintly for a very brief time. "Would you go and bring me some food and drink?"

She needed time to decide if she could trust Ashlax. When he had promised his support and invoked Larcia's name, there had been no stirring of power to suggest that he was lying. The fact was she still didn't like him. That he detested Stacion at least gave them a common enemy. Therefore a truce would exist. She would use him when the time was right, but until then she would tell him only the things he needed to know – when they were needed.

Ashlax did not speak again until after Jai had gone to help with the preventative dosing of so far still healthy children. He spoke mentally as Jai had admonished.

"Jai Mistress, there is a matter about which I must speak. It is of grave importance and concerns the young sorcerer."

Jai ignored him, speaking instead to the girl child she held. "You must drink this little warrior. It is medicine."

"It tastes yuk and I am not a warrior," the girl retorted, spitting out the first mouthful.

"You wriggle like a warrior," Jai told her sternly. "You complain like one. They would rather be stoic about being sick day after day for weeks than take something to stop it."

"Yuk! Don't like being sick."

"Drink this then," Jai ordered, watching the face the girl pulled as she obeyed. Jai gave her some sweet flavoured gum to chew and the girl went off happy.

"Later, Ashlax," Jai told her slave. "I'm almost finished. Go and fill the pool in my cave with water."

Bernea brought her a mug of the herbal brew. "The eldest mother insists that we all have some," she reported. "Even though spotted fever is a whelp's disease."

Jai sniffed at the clay cup and realised that it was different to the cup of preventative medicine she had had with her lunch. This was simply a restorative drink.

"I'm sorry about before," Bernea said quietly. "I shouldn't have asked. It's just that when Con and I... it was wonderful. We risked it because...someone was so intent on you...I'm sorry."

"No Ber, I am. You're my friend. I am just not used to such female talk."

"I had hoped you would like it," Bernea admitted. "Since we did – Con seems surer of himself."

Jai felt a shiver of warning. She had noticed that change but had thought only someone who knew Con well would see it. Maybe Bernea was that close to him. Maybe.

Chapter 22

Ashlax had done more that fill the pool with water; he had added scented oils and found soft towels. A drink was on a wooden try beside the pool.

Jai had never had such luxury. Slaves would never do more than asked, and she had never yearned for such things.

"I'm impressed," Jai said aloud. "Was this all your idea, Ashlax?"

He shook his head in the negative, but said, "Are you pleased, mistress Jai?"

"Yes. All it needs now is for food to arrive. I'm so tired."

"That is organised, Mistress Jai," Ashlax assured her.

When a pouting Siluci brought in the food carrier, Jai was sure of whose orders Ashlax was acting on. She sighed as Siluci departed very quickly.

Jai ate quickly and then drank the prepared drink. She tasted and identified the herbs brewed into it. Soon its effect became apparent. It roused desire in her and also gave her mind a numbing fuzziness.

It was enough so that she didn't care when Stacion Ansuni walked in to observe the activity and linger to harvest the released energy. It was not enough to stop her reasoning, or for her to forget to make it appear that she was the driving force of the mating. When Stacion finally wandered out of the cave, Jai relaxed and let Ashlax bring her up to a state of pleasant ecstasy.

He withdrew and lay next to her where he could whisper in her ear. Jai carefully blocked her mind, so that Stacion would only sense a continuation of her current state and mood.

"He insisted," Ashlax apologised.

Jai shrugged. "What did you want to tell me earlier?"

"That you need to warn the young sorcerer," Ashlax said at once.

"Why?"

"He's going to challenge, isn't he?"

"Not yet," Jai said.

"It had better be soon, before Stacion notices the change in him," Ashlax warned.

"Change?" Jai prompted, feeling afraid.

"His body language – it's not subservient. I hadn't heard that he had been presented for the dreaming and the testing – but he is like those who have received their secret name. Stacion will notice."

"I will warn him," Jai promised. "I did not realise the change was so noticeable."

"Come and bathe," Ashlax suggested. "It will clear your head."

Jai was agreeable to that but declined Ashlax's offer to bathe her. Instead he donned his slave's robe that hid his small wings and stood guard at the cave entrance.

When she was finished and attired for the company of others, Ashlax returned to her. He gestured that he wanted to talk and Jai adjusted the mind shield again, to seem as if she was sweeping the cave.

"Another thing," Ashlax said softly. "I haven't seen that other one - the older apprentice - around."

"Lancho? He's not."

"Do you know where he is?"

Jai shrugged.

"Then you should be sure," he advised. "In a confrontation, the elder can pull on power from his apprentices. The other might appear at an inopportune time."

Jai nodded. Con had probably thought about Lancho but she would see if he knew where their half-brother was.

"Yes, we must find Lancho," Con agreed, his mind full of other matters since Jai had told him what Ashlax had said. "Can you talk to your friend?"

"Yes, but I doubt that Suzi or her brother will be able to find Lancho — not when he is changed. Stacion will have made a good job of it. Whatever he has Lancho doing is too important to him and they don't have our sense of smell. We could pick him by that."

"Then you will have to…" Con stopped when he saw Jai was about to object. "Alright — there has to be another way."

He thought for a time. "Do you think that you can get Jenha to let you near that warrior their father has as a prisoner?"

"That would be dangerous," Jai warned. "But what are you thinking?"

"I can't see how he would still be loyal to Stacion," Con proposed. "So?"

"If we can get the Kumatan to let him lose to find Lancho — for us — or them — it doesn't matter so long as Lancho is neutralised…"

"What if that prisoner is still a yes-man for him?"

"Then we will need to change his mind," Con told her.

"I like the idea," Jai admitted, "Even if it is risky but I don't think I can convince Jenha's father."

Con drummed his fingers on his thigh.

"The Kumatan have started testing our boundaries again. I had to toss half a dozen of their guards back across the river. Later, I spoke to Jenha. He was skulking around trying to surprise me. He mentioned that his father was busy trying to find out about a lot of attacked women. He was tracing various trader groups…"

"Do you think Lancho…?"

"It's not impossible," Con suggested. "Perhaps you could make it a favour to him that you get his prisoner to help him?"

Jai smiled. "I can work with that, I will have to plan to be absent for a while. Now that I have convinced Stacion that I am obeying him and mating with that slave he might relax his watch on me."

"Be wary of that slave," Con warned. "I still don't trust him."

"Nor do I, but we have a truce based on a common hatred," Jai admitted. "He is still intelligent and observant. I have stopped him being able to manipulate the aura – that is all. I don't know if he realises that I didn't complete the disempowering ritual. He shares his observations with me, knowing I will tell you. We – I mean you – might be able to make use of him."

"I don't think I would dare," Con said.

"He can still accumulate power passively," Jai explained. "I can control him – like an apprentice. I can use his power and if needed, pass it to you."

Con snarled a grin and nodded.

"I would rather you kept him close – would he be your body guard?"

"Bro – I do not like him that much! He is around me like a rash as it is."

"Think on it," Con advised. "And remember what I said. Keep all of your important stuff with you. If things turn against me – the land and my tribe will follow you."

"No!" Jai protested. "You cannot lose. Not with me helping you."

"Promise, Jai. If I fail – you must kill him."

"That I will promise. And you had better get Bernea away. What if you got her with egg?"

Con nodded. "You had better get back."

Jai returned to the tribe's village by walking to her cave. Ashlax scrambled to his feet. He was sporting new grazes on his face.

"Some warriors were enquiring after you, Mistress."

"What did you tell them," Jai asked.

"Nothing, Mistress. I am only a slave. My mistress does not tell me her business."

"I had thought those watchers would have been recalled." Jai muttered. "Anyway, thanks for the distraction. Go find something to do. I have to talk to the Elder Mothers."

Jai knew that Ashlax was following her still, but at a further distance. She sighed. It was very annoying. Still, he would hang back when she talked to the mothers.

The mothers welcomed her and agreed to assemble to listen to her. While the word was being spread, Bernea came to sit beside Jai.

"You really must go from here," Jai urged her friend.

"No. I am no coward." Bernea refused.

"I didn't say you were. I was thinking that if Con got you with egg – you and the child would be in great danger."

"I will support Con, no matter the risk."

"And risk a child of Con's?"

"It is too soon to know if there is one," Bernea replied. "Even so, we have pledged to each other, but if I die, he'll choose another to mother his children."

"Damn it, Ber. I hope then that Larcia will continue to protect bird-brained fools."

"For your sake too," Bernea smiled. "I hope she does. You are in greater danger than me."

"I know," Jai admitted. "But my stake in this is personal. If Con fails – I promised him that I would finish the job."

Jai waited until all the old mothers, unmated women and healers had assembled. Then she prayed to Larcia to find the right words to say and for the women the wisdom to make the right decision.

If she had understood the women all these years, they would listen and consider her words. If not she risked their anger and dismissal and even Stacion's punishment.

"A time of division is coming," Jai began, and the nods of all, told them that they understood that a confrontation between Stacion and Con was inevitable.

"The young one is an idealist," the Eldest Mother told her.

Jai nodded, agreeing. "Yes, and I believe the elder was one, once."

Again nods. They waited for her to continue.

"You may consider me biased against the elder, for what he has made me," Jai went on. "But I speak not for myself but for the good of the tribe and for the good of all Atapi and all of Korvu."

"Continue," the Eldest Mother said.

"I ask of you only that some of you consider leaving here – now if possible, soon if you can, to become part of the redeemed ones."

"You assume the younger will win the challenge," another elder spoke. "If so, tradition allows him to choose who will go with him."

"I must believe that the younger will win," Jai stated. "I cannot but doubt that the elder will allow that choice."

"We will each consider," the Eldest Mother directed. "But what if the younger loses? What will happen to the redeemed ones?"

Jai took a deep breath. "I will lead them."

The silence of the women became pronounced. It was as if they had all stopped breathing.

Finally, the Eldest Mother stated, "You are not a sorcerer."

"Larcia led a tribe," Jai stated in turn.

"Truth. Do you claim to speak with her voice, child?" the Eldest Mother challenged.

Jai shook her head. "Larcia still exists in the aura of the Rock of Arkor. She welcomed me there. If tradition did not bar women from there she would welcome each of you. She took me there. She taught me that once the three races of Korvu were in balance – leaders, administrators, fighters. All important. All equal. Atapi and Kumatan should not fight each other. Atapi should not fight Atapi. Atapi sorcerers should not warp the aura for their own ends – but work with it."

"Heresy," a younger woman proclaimed.

"Truth," the Eldest Mother confirmed. "What then do you see that we Atapi must fight?"

"Alien beings," Jai said.

There was a quiet babble as the women reacted to that notion.

"From where? How do you know that beings exist away from here?" Jai was asked.

"Two hundred years ago – the sorcerer Loschak died. He was killed by beings that had weapons of metal and fire. Larcia led me to his bones – I took his memory box to the Rock."

The muttering indicated that not all believed her.

"Silence!" the Eldest Mother ordered. "The Kumatan have long traded with beings from other worlds. Nothing that they have gained from such alliances has ever been shared with us. However, if greed and avarice can exist in Atapi – other peoples could easily be the same."

Jai spoke her final words. "I have chosen to protect my world from invaders. For the races that belong here, even if the Kumatan and Kimh despise us."

The Eldest Mother indicated for Jai to leave. She obeyed; sure that she had the support of the Eldest Mother. She didn't know if the powerful old woman would choose to stay or to go. It would be her decision as to how she felt she could best serve the Atapi. Each of the women would decide that for herself.

Bernea had decided. She walked with Jai as they left the women's area. Neither spoke until they were near the open gathering area. It was mostly deserted. The only women in sight were minding the children. These were those who would have to follow their mates' allegiance. They had not been invited to the meeting.

Chapter 23

A movement near her shielded cave caused Jai to look that way. At first, she thought it was just Ashlax, although why he would be there, she wasn't sure. Then she realised that he was struggling with someone who looked pale skinned.

Jai grabbed Bernea's arm, and after a quick glance around, dragged her three steps forward to arrive next to Ashlax.

A start of surprise escaped from Bernea when she realised that Jai could do the sorcerer's walk.

"Let her go, Ashlax," Jai directed.

"But she's…"

"She is not a threat."

"But she…"

Jai allowed the cave entrance to be visible for a moment and pushed Ashlax and his captive inside. Bernea followed, after checking to see if anyone had seen them suddenly arrive there.

"Auslak, you have not seen a stranger. This is Galli, daughter of Worrall."

The command took hold. If asked, that is what Ashlax would say. His expression was however, calculating.

"Wait outside," Jai ordered. He obeyed and from watching him, Jai knew he would try to listen. His expression, clearly visible from within the cave, showed his anger when he realised that he could not re-enter the cave, and that the entrance now seemed to be solid rock.

Bernea had gone at once to Suzi Mosellan who had collapsed into a sobbing heap on the floor. It took a while to calm her down enough to understand her.

Finally, Jai transformed into her Kumatan form, so Suzi could speak in her normal language.

Suzi had been with a group of Kimh girls, with guards nearby. They had been visiting the trader's market and some of the off-world traders were there. Suzi had wanted to see if any of them had brought more "cats". She had recognised these traders from earlier visits.

After leaving that booth, another trader had come to offer his wares. This wasn't an unusual practice and he had attractive jewellery and perfume. He had deftly shepherded her out of sight of the guards and then grabbed her roughly. Then he had begun to make obscene suggestions.

"He spoke Kumatan," Suzi said. "A bit oddly, but it's what he said. It was the same stuff that … that Atapi said to me before we escaped from here. Exactly. And he knew me – he said so."

Jai swore in Atapi. "Lancho," she finished.

"He dragged me into one of those trader wagons – it was padded – he said no one would be able to hear me scream." Suzi went on. "But I could walk a bit inside and I remembered how you had taken me back and I thought I could do it. I did, but I ended up here."

Jai wondered briefly if Larcia had again interfered a "little".

"Suzi – the traders you knew – do you know their names? Do you think they knew Lancho? Do you know where they bring goods from? Are they always at that market? What was their wagon like? The one Lancho put you in?"

Although overwhelmed by the questions, Suzi's mind recalled vividly the earlier events and Jai shared it.

Jai didn't quite know what to do next. She had the means to find Lancho but could do nothing to stop him. She couldn't involve Con – he was jumping to Stacion's demands.

"Why didn't you go to your father? He is the best one to stop Lancho."

"He's busy," Suzi began. "And I wasn't meant to go to the traders."

"But he needs to know," Jai thought quickly. "Ber, tell Ashlax to get a bath ready for me. I have to do some practice rituals here for a bit and maybe meditate."

Bernea guessed otherwise but said nothing.

When she had gone, she spoke to Suzi. "I'll go back with you. You will have to get someone to contact your father. And you will have to admit what you did – sneaking out and then coming to me. You can say coming here was an accident. I will tell him it was a lucky one because if Lancho is changed, I can still find him. And your father can have him when I do."

"But she is not lying, Traeger Mosellan. Nor am I. She came as she said." Jai had used the honorific title that she had heard others use. None of those others had realised that she was an Atapi in their form.

Jellarn Mosellan was angry at what he considered an ill-timed summons. He had hardly listened to what Suzi had said. To distract him, Jai had briefly changed back into her own shape only to be immediately grabbed by two guards.

"Listen to your child, Traeger Mosellan," Jai insisted, not trying to free herself. "She has the key to the problem you have and it was lucky that she came to me. In this matter – I want to help. I want Lancho out of the way. I want him where he can't act on his perverted desires. You find him and control him and you win. I win."

"Very well," Jellarn Mosellan conceded, indicating that his guards could release Jai. She immediately returned to Kumatan shape.

"Tell me what happened again, Suzelaine," Jellarn Mosellan, forcing himself to calm.

This time he questioned her to get every possible piece of information.

"We will talk about this again," Jellarn Mosellan told his daughter. "And about how you managed to reach a place that is fifty miles away."

His tone implied that such a feat was impossible for a girl, that she must have had help.

"Both of you will stay here while I organise a search."

Here – was a room in the Royal Palace and Jai felt far from comfortable.

"Do you think he will find him," Jai asked, wanting to leave.

"He can call on as much help as he needs," Suzi told her.

"He should have let me help," Jai insisted.

"He says that he knows every trick ever thought about by Atapi sorcerers," Suzi boasted.

"Maybe he does," Jai allowed. "But do you think he knew we could change shape before I did it in front of him?"

"I heard him talking to my uncle. I think he knew it was possible but had never seen it. I think he thought it was a myth. Why?"

"Because I don't think that he will be able to find Lancho. He can hide himself when he doesn't want to be seen and I think Stacion might have made the change fixed."

"And what could you do?" Suzi asked.

"Smell him," was her unexpected reply. "I don't think Kumatan have noses as sensitive as ours."

"What do you mean?"

"Atapi have a particular smell. You Kumatan don't. I don't normally notice it when I am around Atapi. Here – I would I think."

"Wouldn't Lancho smell you too?" Suzi considered.

"Not if I put on that smell of yours – the flower one," Jai suggested. "And he would never expect an Atapi woman here – changed. It is assumed that the ability is restricted to sorcerers or males – but I think we could all do it if we had to."

Suzi was thoughtful. "You are right he smelt – unwashed – but nothing distinctive."

Jai tried to wait patiently, but was feeling very edgy, knowing that she needed to get back to the village before she was missed. "How long do you think he will be? I need to get back."

Suzi shrugged. "He won't take kindly to me asking."

Jai sighed.

Jellarn Mosellan, with his son Jenha, returned before Jai tried to leave by herself. But barely.

"Gone," Jenha told his sister. "The other traders know the one we wanted, but he's gone."

"Jai thinks she can find him," Suzi blurted.

"How?" Jellarn Mosellan snapped.

Jai didn't answer. She was feeling very weird.

Suzi repeated what Jai had said, all the while watching her friend.

"We'll try it," Jellarn Mosellan decided. "Before the trail gets cold."

He took, Jai's arm, but she didn't seem aware of him.

"What's wrong?" he asked her impatiently.

She heard him and tried to explain. "My energy is ebbing and surging."

"Change back to Atapi," Jenha suggested.

Jai shook her head. "I think – Stacion is about to challenge Con. And I think he is trying to pull me there."

"Who? Con?" Jenha asked.

"No. Stacion. He won't want me to help Con and I promised Con that I would."

"I didn't think Atapi tradition allowed females to be involved in challenges," Jellarn Mosellan commented.

"I don't care," Jai almost snarled. "It's the end result that matters."

Jellarn Mosellan smiled. "I'd support that – yet you would not want this Lancho to help Stacion, would you? Is that why you were so keen to have him found?"

Jai nodded. "But I have to go. I am being torn. He is forcing me to come. Like he did to Suzi."

"No. Find Lancho, and then you can go. Stacion's power is not as strong as mine in this place."

"Father!" Jenha protested. "Look at her. Keeping her here is torturing her."

"Then what do you suggest, boy?" Jellarn Mosellan snarled.

Jenha had no idea until one came unbidden.

"Your prisoner, Obaki," Jenha suggested. "Could you make him do it?"

It was Jellarn Mosellan's turn to be thoughtful. "What if he is still loyal to Stacion?"

"Let me talk to him," Jai offered, her voice a hiss of pain.

Making an instant decision, Jellarn nodded. In doing so, deciding to trust Jai.

He had Jenha hold Jai's other arm and the three of them 'walked' to his house, leaving Suzi at the palace.

As soon as they arrived, Jenha removed Jai's stone from his pocket and pressed it into her hand. She felt the stored power in it rushing into her. Though if Stacion kept dragging at her the mini power relic would soon be drained. She put the stone away when she felt strong enough to resist Stacion for a time. As they walked along a passage, Jai regained her own shape.

Obaki, the aging ex-warrior, jumped to his feet as Jellarn Mosellan entered. His greeting stopped mid-word when he saw Jai helped into the room. His mouth dropped open, when the Kumatan released her.

Jai drew more power from her stone and took a deep breath.

"Obaki, warrior of tribe Ansuni. I am Jai Ansuni, child of Stacion Ansuni, womb mate of Con Ansuni. Do you know me?"

Obaki nodded, nervously. He feared that his cowardice, his worthlessness for not escaping was about to be punished.

"Child of Stacion – I plead mercy. I do not deserve to live." Obaki threw himself at Jai's feet.

"May I judge that," Jai asked gently.

The unexpected question caused Obaki to look up.

"I am not here for Stacion Ansuni," Jai explained. "If you returned to the tribe – Stacion would indeed order your death. Do you think he still knows you are alive?"

Obaki shook his head, awkwardly because of his lowly posture.

"How long have you been here?" Jai asked.

"Many seasons, Mistress," was all he could say.

"Have they treated you well?"

"Yes, except that I cannot be free."

"In that time have you tried to teach the Kumatan to understand the Atapi?" Jai asked - giving what she expected was the truth another interpretation.

"I…yes," Obaki agreed, moving from his almost prone posture to a crouch.

Jai began to feel the drag on her again and clutched the stone again.

"Obaki, I have a request. Will you swear loyalty to Con Ansuni, through me, who shares the same blood? Or do you wish to remain loyal to one who has made no attempt to rescue you and who thinks you dead?"

"Mistress, I am unfit to serve any master. Stacion would be right to kill me."

"Con and I do not agree. A dead warrior is of no use to anyone. You are alive and we have need of a warrior who will grant the Kumatan respect and serve also the needs of the Atapi. Will you undertake a task for Con Ansuni and earn back your honour as a warrior?"

Obaki glanced at Jellarn Mosellan, who nodded slightly. Jai noticed the gesture.

"Yes, Mistress." Obaki stood up, bowed to Jai and repeated a vow of obedience to Con Ansuni.

"An Atapi of Stacion's tribe is committing atrocities on Kumatan women," Jai explained to Obaki.

"He is changed to look like one of us. Jai Ansuni believes you can help find him," Jellarn Mosellan added.

A long denied chance to hunt excited Obaki and put a new light in his eyes.

"Changed? He is a sorcerer then?" Obaki queried.

"Not yet," Jai corrected. "But he has some skills. He can hide himself from Kumatan – but I doubt that he can hide from an Atapi warrior. He will still smell like an Atapi."

Obaki's snarl sounded fierce.

"I would need clothing to hide myself in," Obaki suggested.

"You prove that your mind is still that of a warrior," Jai praised him. "But there might be a better way."

"Do you mean, he changes shape," Jenha blurted. "Is it possible? Isn't that a sorcerer talent?"

Jai shrugged. "Things I have heard suggest it is a latent talent in all Atapi. I have done it and no one taught me." The words were for Obaki's benefit.

"You are not exactly a common example," Jellarn Mosellan said thoughtfully. "Yet, if it can be done it would be a more tactful way. Less noticeable. Can you bind him in that form?"

Jai shook her head. "I have no idea how to do that. Do you?"

"I think so," Jellarn Mosellan considered. "It is a very old ritual. It is reversible. However, I dislike the idea of having Atapi that look like us roaming freely."

Obaki surprised the two Kumatan by speaking up.

"Master, I promised to respect you and your kind. I will regain no honour by running off. Nor would there be anywhere to run to. This is my chance to repay your kindness. However, I would not resent it if you insisted on one of yours accompanying me to teach me how to act like one of yours."

Jellarn Mosellan almost smiled. "You are wily indeed, and wise, Obaki. I will not underestimate you."

Obaki bowed.

Jai felt the need to hurry. She quickly explained how it was that she had first changed. In a surprisingly short time, Obaki had the knack. The Jai explained rapidly in her own language all she knew about what Lancho was doing both for himself and for Stacion. She mentioned which things that the Traeger did not know, implying no need to inform him of things that were tribe business only. She told him to report to Jellarn if he found Lancho so that the Traeger could neutralise him, but stressed the information that was vital to her.

She passed the stone Jenha had returned to her to Obaki. "If you have news for me, hold the stone and think of me. I will come if I can."

"Mistress, willingly, and with the Master's approval I will do this for Con Ansuni. May he win his own tribe."

Jai gave a sigh of relief. Relaxing even that much was a mistake for at that moment she felt the power dragging at her, catch her, and pull.

Chapter 24

Stacion growled his success as Jai appeared before him, and he grabbed her before she realised he was behind her. He sniffed her.

"Traitor! You reek of my enemies," Stacion snarled, baring his teeth.

That moment of distraction was all Jai needed to shield her mind from him.

"I will deal with you after I have swatted that excrescence that shared a womb with you. It won't take long and then you will know what it feels like to have your eyes burnt out, your ears punctured, your tongue cut out, your hands and feet chopped off and what is left thrown in the desert as food for the scavengers."

The malevolent glitter in his eyes convinced Jai that he meant every word.

"Ashlax!" Stacion roared. The slave trotted quickly to his presence and bowed with his head touching the ground.

"Take this woman to her cave. Ensure that she stays there. If she leaves, you will share her fate. I will not have a female interfering in my business."

Jai permitted Ashlax to hustle her away. Her legs felt like would not hold her weight. She knew that Stacion was about to challenge Con. She had to warn him.

She felt Stacion trying to compel her silence and obedience. He wanted to prevent her from warning Con. Did he know of their bond? Or was he being paranoid?

It didn't matter. Con was warned. She had called him as soon as Stacion had grabbed her. Amazingly, after a moment of alarm, his mind had become calm.

In the cave, Ashlax released her, but grabbed again when Jai tried to leave.

"You dare not be seen by him, he is beyond reason," Ashlax warned.

Jai snarled. "He has been beyond reason for a long time. And I promised – promised – I would support Con in this."

"It isn't permitted!" Ashlax almost yelled. "Should you interfere - the Old One will award the battle against the one you help."

"What does the Old One have to do with this?" Jai snarled.

Ashlax did not look like a cowed slave. "He will know when the battle starts. He and others will come to ensure tradition is followed."

"It is not his business," Jai hissed.

"He has made it so. He and the other sorcerers have excluded Stacion. They have barred him from the Rock of Arkor."

"How…do you…know…this?" Jai hissed slowly. She glared at her slave. "You have been keeping them informed – spying on us."

"Yes," Ashlax admitted bluntly. "I came to destroy him and failed – because of you. You mastered me, but did not destroy me. I cannot use magic but I can sense it and I still have my mind and knowledge. I can help you."

"If they wanted rid of him, why would they stop me helping Con?"

"Because once it becomes a formal challenge – it must follow tradition."

"Let me out! I will kill him before Con comes. Before it is a challenge."

"He would swat you dead," Ashlax told her bluntly. "And then he would challenge Con. Think, Mistress. If you are not seen – no one will realise you are helping."

"If I am not seen, slave, I cannot see to help."

"Mistress, I was not forbidden to watch. Stacion does not command me. Because we mated, and you can watch my mind - you can view events through my eyes. No one outside of this cave, except Con, knows your full power. So – if you are not seen, no one will believe that you can interfere."

Jai saw the deadly logic in what Ashlax said. "And if Lancho appears?"

"If he interferes, then Con will win. But Stacion knows that. I am surprised that he sent you out of the way."

Jai calmed down. "He isn't thinking straight." In fact, Stacion had always been blind to her power.

"No," Ashlax agreed. "The smell of Kumatan enraged him. The Circle of Sorcerers will also ensure they do not interfere."

A roar like thunder reverberated even inside her cave. Jai had never heard the like.

"The call to challenge," Ashlax told her. "The challenger has the choice of battle ground."

Jai reached for Con's mind and she sensed the answering roar in her brother's mind. It was less forceful, less confident, but still strongly determined. In a brief aside, directed at her he sent, "Keep Bernea safe."

Moments later, Bernea scuttled into the cave and ran to Jai and clung to her.

They both knew what was happening. There was no need for words. After a moment, Jai pushed her friend away.

"We must be strong," Jai told her. Bernea nodded.

"I will," she said stoutly. "But I couldn't stay away."

Jai took Bernea's hand and squeezed gently. "Can you go and warn the Elder Mothers?"

"They know. After you left the meeting, those that chose to swear to Con, did so. Con took them to his land."

"And you?" Jai asked.

"In my heart, I have."

"Why didn't you go?" Jai asked.

"I couldn't," Bernea said, hiding her face. "Stacion had me waiting on him. He…"

A sob escaped her. "He claimed me for a mate. He…told me I was to be Lancho's after he had finished with me."

Jai's anger flared again. Not because Stacion had exercised his tribal sorcerer's prerogative to mate with any woman he wanted but because he had done it to deliberately goad Con.

Ashlax had been watching from the opening. "Con's here."

But Jai already knew. Her mind was linked to Con, aware of everything he thought and felt, but shielded so Stacion would not sense her.

"So the would-be sorcerer thinks he can beat me," Stacion spat at Con, as he stalked around. "Do you really think a wet-hided whelp like you – at the wise age of seventeen summers, can defeat me?"

Con grinned and began to strut around Stacion. "Why not? I learnt from a master. I am not an imbecile like Lancho and you know he will never be welcomed at Arkor – any more than you are now."

Stacion tried to overpower Con's mind, but Con was prepared. Stacion hissed in anger, realising that the master-apprentice bond was broken.

Con grinned even wider. "Yes, old tired has-been. I have been welcomed at Arkor, sat the night vigil. I have my secret name."

Stacion seemed to realise that Con was circling him, not vice-versa, and leapt off the ground. He made it seem like he was going to land on Con, but the younger sorcerer was no longer in the same position. Con "walked" to a position behind Stacion, and in a flicker of movement, swept a knife from a belt sheath and slashed Stacion's wings. Stacion twirled, but Con had vanished.

"Coward!" Stacion roared, but in that instant, a knife stabbed into his side. Stacion sealed the wound with a surge of power.

In the cave, Ashlax murmured to Bernea who was staring intently at Jai's face. "They will be exchanging insults and testing each other for weaknesses."

Jai heard him and added, "Stacion's ego is his weakest point."

"Don't underestimate him," Ashlax warned. "He has fought in many such fights and this is for the highest stakes yet. His life. His right to rule a tribe. His honour and status. If Con wins – his position will be lower than all the other sorcerers because Con is the lowest ranking one now. Con, if he wins, will inherit Stacion's tribe. If Con fails, Stacion will keep his tribe."

Jai kept part of her mind with Con, but let her senses feel the aura. It was swirling about both combatants.

Stacion could not block Con from it for Con was of Stacion's blood. The land was in Con's blood because he was born to it. Con was instantly aware when Stacion began to warp the aura to use it in a ritual.

Con began a ritual of his own, calling up a swarm of biting, stinging insects. It was a slow building piece of sorcery that worked with the aura, not forcing it.

Stacion continued to taunt Con with his inexperience, his age, for being a wing-less worm, for his ultimate failure – trying to provoke an angry response. Con simply continued to grin, savouring his own secrets, waiting to taste the nectar of victory when Stacion realised that he had lost more than half his tribe and was blocked from countless power artefacts.

Another, older sorcerer might have reacted to the insults but Con had not yet developed an inflated ego. He knew his wings were small. He knew it would be a century or so before they grew big enough to bear him in flight. But wings - huge and powerful like Stacion's could also be a disadvantage. They made him a bigger target.

The whirlwind sprang into existence from nowhere, sucking dirt and leaves into its vortex. It screamed towards Con who appeared to continue circling Stacion and be ignorant of its approach.

Con was aware of it, felt Jai in his mind, working through him to form a healer's shield as she had done against the snakes. Being sure of her skill and strength, he concentrated on his own magic, bringing the insects, and sending them to the focus of the warped energy. Stacion had sprung aloft, crowing with the danger he thought Con was unaware of. When the insects struck, he fell, writhing to the ground. When he used power to blast them all dead, he lost control of the whirlwind. Con neatly took it over and sent it towards Stacion.

Ashlax was watching the two battling sorcerers and telling Bernea what was happening.

"He is draining energy from me," Bernea said, she was lying limply on the ground.

"The Old One is here," Ashlax said almost with a gulp. "And the others, all eighteen of them. They are forming a circle to contain the battle. Stacion has just flicked the whirlwind away from himself. Con is sending it back again but it is losing intensity."

After a while, "He's got a sword from somewhere! No! It's a long knife. He is attacking Con with it. Con has only got a short knife."

Jai contracted her 'healer's shield' around Con – to give him room to fight.

She clenched her teeth; she had never seen that long knife before. It wasn't the one that had been made from the leech blade. In this she could do little to influence things. She must trust Con's skill with a blade.

For what seemed an endless time, Con and Stacion parried and thrust with neither gaining an advantage. Con had cast an illusion so that Stacion saw him with a long blade as well as a knife. It forced Stacion to jump back to protect himself. Con pressed his advantage and scored yet another scratch on Stacion. It was a deeper wound this time, coming away purple with blood. The knife seemed to rouse in Con's hand, like an animal twisting to attack.

That moment of distraction gave Stacion an opening and he slashed with the long knife then stabbed with a short one.

Jai quickly chanted a ritual for healing cuts. She felt power draining from Con. The long knife was a leech blade.

Con recognised the drain on his energy and reacted immediately with a series of moves that betrayed his true skill and suggested that until then he had only been playing at blade fighting.

Con saw the new 'respect' in Stacion's eyes. It filled Jai with pride. The knife Con used, Loschak's knife – drew more blood from Stacion. It had a life of its own, parrying Stacion's thrusts and scoring cut after cut on Stacion's chest. The rich fabric Stacion had dressed in was cut to ribbons and soaked in blood.

Stacion withdrew to the edge of the circle of battle and roared defiance. Jai felt him trying to compel her to come to him. Bernea began to crawl to the cave door; she had no energy to walk. Jai tried to stop her, grabbing her legs and holding fast. Bernea was trying to struggle. In the next instant, the form that was Bernea vanished and Jai was holding nothing.

"Stacion has her," Ashlax reported. "It looks like he is sending her for refreshments."

"Is that allowed?" Jai asked.

"Con can do it too, if he dares."

"I would like to make a scorpion nest appear under him," Jai muttered.

"Too easy," Ashlax countered. "He would blast it and it would be gone. Illusion would be better."

"Illusions don't bite," Jai retorted. "Look at him! Flaunting his wings like a giant bat."

Con was taking a moment to collect his thoughts, aware that his energy was draining from him. He had not expected that knife. He had assumed that Stacion would use his newest weapon. It only needed to touch blood to do to Stacion what Stacion's other blade was doing to him.

Bernea raced back – carrying a skin of liquid. Stacion flicked out his hand and grabbed her. Bernea fought to free herself, making Stacion grin fiercely. Stacion spoke to her but the sound didn't carry.

Bernea did what Stacion was not expecting. She drew a knife, a small sharp blade and slashed his arm. Stacion grabbed it with his free hand and crowed.

"You saw that!" he yelled to the ring of sorcerers. "This female tried to help my worthless whelp. I claim victory."

Jai slumped in dismay, as one of the ring of watchers approached.

"The Old One," Ashlax reported, letting Jai close enough to the entrance to see for herself.

The question put to Bernea could be heard throughout the village.

"Why did you take the part of the challenged, woman? It is forbidden."

Bernea faced the Old One and drew herself up.

"It was not the challenged that drew me across planes to fetch him water."

"But you attacked the challenger, woman. In that you helped the other."

"I did not! I attacked to help myself," Bernea proclaimed, her voice amplified by sorcery. "I would not let him harm me again. Before this challenge, he mated with me to bind me to him. He did it to spite the challenged. "

"It is his right," the Old One stated. "He is the leader of your tribe."

"He has no right, when I am already mated to another and bearing an egg to that other."

The Old One looked at Bernea with mingled respect and antagonism. He chanted a ritual and stared at Bernea. It proved to him that she was telling the truth.

Before the Old One could pronounce judgement, Stacion drew his jewelled knife and slashed Bernea across the throat and tossed her aside.

He stared at the Old One. "I have judged that female a traitor to my tribe and pronounced judgement."

Stacion dared the Old One to object.

"The challenge continues," the Old One pronounced, before stalking away.

Jai stared at the point where Bernea lay and her mind prayed to Larcia to preserve her.

Chapter 25

Con was staring at the same place, his mind seething with anger. Jai thought at him.

"Be calm – trust Larcia. He wants you angry. It is a point against him that a woman scored on him. And remember, he used that jewelled knife on her. Her blood! She is bound to you where it matters, in her heart."

"Yes!" Con hissed. "Now I can control it."

Con stalked towards Stacion. He now carried a real sword, summoned by sorcery.

Stacion stalked to meet him.

"A lesson to you, worm. All those in this village are mine to do with as I please. I taught her who her real master was."

Con ignored the mention of Bernea. "I doubt that all the people here are yours." He shrugged in the direction of the Old One.

"Don't you care that I killed your female? Your mate? Your egg?"

Con answered calmly. "When I have shown you how useless you have become – all the women here will be mine. I'll take another." He shrugged. "Perhaps Siluci will prefer a strong young warrior sorcerer to a debauched, slack fleshed ancient. I will take her whelp for my own – or I could have it killed."

Instead of inflaming Con to thoughtless anger, Stacion had it turned on him. Con realised with a shiver of premonition that Stacion did not like losing anything he thought of as his.

Stacion began to gyrate, raising a vortex of wind in front of him. The vortex began to move towards Con, drawing in all kinds of debris. Con moved, but the vortex followed him unerringly.

Jai had no idea what Con was doing when he first ran through the village, leaping over the embers in the unattended fire pits and then racing towards the river.

Stacion was laughing like a demented evil spirit.

Jai sensed that Con had a purpose, a way to win against the wind, but no idea of a ritual to counter the 'winning' effect of this attack in the minds of the 'judges'.

All Jai could think to do was to distract Stacion somehow and reduce his control of the wind.

"I wonder what creatures haunt his nightmares," Ashlax pondered aloud as he watched Stacion's performance. "If he keeps this up he will kill everything for miles around. The aura around here is almost fully depleted."

Then Jai knew. In that instant of knowing, Con knew exactly what would scare Stacion.

The vortex had taken up embers and was now a fiery tornado, visible above the trees and it was setting fire to all the trees which were dry and brittle from having the life drained from them. The trees became a wall of flame.

The watching sorcerers had moved away from the vortex.

"They will only let him out of the circle for a short time," Ashlax warned.

But Con knew that. He raced to the river. It was only flowing sluggishly because it to was being drained of the aura. As soon as he was sure that the vortex would reach the river, he 'walked' across planes, back to the village.

Stacion had slumped to his knees, as power was leeched from him. He didn't seem to be noticing the drain. He still clutched his favourite knife and his eyes glittered with a sense of triumph.

Ashlax nudged Jai and pointed to a figure creeping closer to the circle of watchers. It was clad in a brown hooded cape. It had the stature of a Kumatan.

"Lancho," Jai breathed just as a sudden gust of wind swept with a roar from the direction of the river. It blew the cowl off figure's head, revealing a pale skinned, big eyed face. The figure staggered in the breeze, clutching something closely to its chest.

The watching sorcerers had stumbled backwards too. They had not expected the force of the warped aura, returning to its natural place.

The fiery vortex had gone. Con had damped it with the flowing water. Now, as she watched the sky, clouds were massing, darkening with moisture and spreading from above the village. Lightning and thunder were present.

Stacion was calling insults to bring Con back to him. He did not see Con walking slowly into the village from behind him. Jai saw him when he walked over to where Bernea lay. He lifted her and walked and vanished.

"Jai – help her," Con pleaded from behind her.

Jai spun around. "I…yes," she answered. She was horrified by Con's state. He was covered with skin abrasions, burns, bleeding scratches and cuts. Then she was overwhelmed by the fact that Bernea was still alive.

Ashlax studied Con's injuries and said bluntly, "You need to end this soon."

"I have had worse from him," Con said. "But you are right."

Con 'walked' back to the area in front of Stacion, but not as himself. He had created an illusion of one of the deadly creatures that had killed Loschak – complete with the seeming of their metal fire breathing weapons.

All he actually had in his hand was Loschak's knife, but as soon as he was close to Stacion something roused again – as if Loschak stood beside him, unseen, unheard, but guiding him.

Con felt his extreme tiredness vanish as he felt a flow of energy feeding him from his distant land. He felt energy coming sluggishly from Stacion through the jewelled knife that had touched the blood of Bernea, his chosen mate – his soul partner, the bearer of his egg.

Stacion turned at the slightest hint of sound – his hackles up. His wings, previously spread wide and proud, closed slightly.

Stacion screamed, and it seemed to be more from fear than for defiance or battle.

Con flicked a stone into his hand, and then sent it shooting at Stacion with a flicker of fire. Stacion stumbled back as if the stone had not merely hit him, but penetrated his flesh. Con continued to pound him with little stones, and Stacion seemed too paralysed by fear to retaliate.

"Master. I have it," a voice shouted out and Stacion's wings flicked wider.

"It does not matter what help Lancho brings, STAK! I have your name. I have your stored power – your relics feed me," Con yelled loudly enough for all the watchers to hear.

Stak froze for a moment, reaching out for his power relics and finding each one blocked or empty.

"You have not won! Worm! Whelp excrescence," Stak roared defiantly. He reached towards Lancho and the item he held flew into his hands. It looked like a carved wooden cup with a narrow neck below it and a round flat base. He held it up above his head and chanted.

Jai was aware of externals, but busy using all her skills to mend the gash in Bernea's neck. With awe she had realised that the knife had not severed any major arteries, or the wind pipe. Larcia had indeed protected her – or the knife had recognised her bond to Con and slipped aside.

Jai heard Con's challenge of victory, and Stacion's refusal to concede. She felt a sensation of being pulled and knew what Stacion was doing. He would kill her – to further punish Con.

"NO! I WILL NOT GO!" Jai screamed in defiance.

Ashlax grabbed her, held her, as a force outside of her began to exert drag on her.

In her mind came Larcia's voice. "You must, child. What Stacion plans – cannot be allowed. You promised – if Con did not kill him – you would."

From outside of the cave, Jai heard a series of explosions – felt the pull on her ease and she pushed Ashlax away. He slumped to the ground. Jai felt herself pulled into blackness – like that of between planes – for what seemed like eternity.

She thought desperately of places she knew, imagined herself walking there, but couldn't move.

She wondered if this was death.

Chapter 26

Con turned slowly around, using every sense he had to try to locate Stak. He breathed in and out in controlled gasps – expecting an unpleasant surprise at any moment.

None came. The threatening thunder and lightning continued. The dark clouds covered the village and beyond.

The power in the storm 'hovered' like something about to explode. The fire burning in the dried trees flared and travelled as a strong wind arose.

Con looked at the storm, quietly spoke a ritual, and the extreme tension in the air snapped. Huge drenching drops of rain began to fall on the village. Con waved his hand and the storm moved to drench the fire.

Gradually, some tiny fraction of the power that Stak had drained from the land, stored in his relics and he had liberated when he had taken that object from Lancho – returned to the aura.

The Old One and the other seventeen tribal sorcerers drew nearer in a circle around Con. He eyed them warily.

"What?" he demanded, facing the Old One. He was the oldest, the highest ranked of all the sorcerers. "Do I have to fight all of you too – to prove I'm good enough? Stak is gone, fled. By the traditions – I have won!"

"You have won," the Old One stated formally. "All here that was once Stacion Ansuni's is now yours. Henceforth, Stacion Ansuni is nameless, is nobody. The aura is denied to him. I sense, however that it is a hollow victory."

Con stared at the Old One, wondering what he meant. The Old One was glancing around and finally focussed on something with a look of distaste.

Looking in the same direction Con saw Ashlax approaching very slowly. He reached out to sense the slave's thoughts. This was something he had only been able to do since Jai had mated with him. The roiling thoughts were laced with guilt. Two thoughts were clear. Jai was gone and all the villagers were gone.

Instinctively, Con reached for Jai's mind - nothing.

He reached out to sense the life of the village. It was too quiet. There was just a vague sense of someone in Jai's cave.

The circle opened to let Ashlax come into speaking distance.

The Old One stared, not at but past Ashlax.

"What?" Con snapped. He was tired, drained and worried.

"Mistress Jai is gone. I tried to keep her here – but she pushed me away. And there is no one around, not warrior, women or whelps. Only the friend of Jai."

"I am aware of that," Con stated. He was secretly elated that Bernea was still around and alive. He turned to the Old One.

"I am a Sorcerer Devil. I have my own tribe. I have my own land. How do I rank amongst you?"

"Where is your tribe?" the Old One demanded.

"On my land. Land once that of Loschak," Con stated.

"Forbidden land! Ill-omened land," the Old One stated.

"No!" Con retorted, drawing Loschak's knife and removing the illusion on it. "Ceded to me."

The Old One reached out for the knife hilt and when he touched it his posture went rigid and his face blank. As the other sorcerers began to move in a threatening manner, the Old One stated, "Con Ansuni ranks where his sire once ranked. In spite of his youth, he has proven himself by overcoming one of great power. By fleeing, his sire has proven unworthy to be ranked amongst us. Tonight we all gather at the sacred Rock of Arkor where the life and death of Loschak and the succession of his heir will be celebrated."

The Old One and all the other sorcerers walked away vanished across planes back to their own lands.

Ashlax fell prone at Con's feet and begged forgiveness.

"For what?" Con asked.

"I tried to keep Jai here, but Stacion was too strong."

"Get up Ashlax," Con invited putting his hand out to help him to his feet.

Ashlax scanned Con's face for a hint of his feelings.

"Why? I am an unworthy slave. I do not deserve to stand in your presence."

Con pulled him up and asked, "One question. Answer honestly. Who put you up to that snake business?"

Ashlax drew himself up and answered, "My sire."

"The Old One?" Con asked. "Don't deny it. He could read your mind."

Ashlax nodded and waited.

"Why?"

"Because Stacion Ansuni had to die. He was putting himself before his tribe – before all Atapi. His actions were endangering us all."

"Your actions endangered innocent Atapi," Con spoke passionately. His voice seemed like a whip cutting through Ashlax, who trembled.

"This is not an excuse, but a reason. The Old One declared Stacion's line tainted. Lancho will never be accepted at the Rock. We believed you to be too young to defeat him. No one wished to have what Stacion had touched."

"Did he doubt the strength of his own blood?" Con spoke in disgust. "If so, then I will challenge him next – for he sired my mother."

Ashlax looked astounded. "I did not know that. But I do not think you should challenge him. He has granted you high rank and he will provide you with protection."

Con snarled. "From all those other 'lesser; sorcerers who will challenge me because he placed me – a young whelp – over them? That is no favour. Still, I will hold him to that. I need time to consolidate what is mine. You may return to him and tell him that I expect his protection from other Sorcerer Devils," Con turned away and strode to where he sensed Bernea.

He lifted her so he could embrace her, but as he held her he sensed Ashlax approaching quietly and squatting a discrete distance away.

"I said you could go," Con snarled, wanting solitude.

"Master, I have nowhere to go," Ashlax admitted with shame. "My sire will not allow me to return. I have no magic and he knows I was defeated."

"But you were in contact with him, passing on everything you learnt." Con accused.

"Yes, Master. I was instructed to pretend to be defeated. And indeed, I fooled Stacion. I did not expect to be defeated by a female. I hid that from him – until he came here. He said I had disgraced him. Let me serve you, Master."

Con though on the offer. Putting aside his hatred for the evil sorcery, he considered how Jai had come to think of him as a useful ally.

"Very well, but not as a slave," Con decided. "And only if you swear loyalty to me and cut ties with the Old One."

"Yes," Ashlax promised. "Can I help you now?"

"I don't know. Bernea is alive, but she will not wake. I prayed to Larcia to protect her."

"Jai Mistress was doing healing on her when…when some force began pulling on her. She didn't want to go – she wanted to save her friend… for you."

"What happened?" Con asked.

"She screamed that she would not go. So I held her, but it was like she was being pulled from me. Then there were explosions outside and she pushed me away. I must have blacked out for I woke up sprawled across her friend and she was gone."

"Is there no one else here? No one at all?" Con asked.

"No one alive. There are two old warriors – dead. But everything else stayed here – all belongings, everything not attached to people."

"He's gone somewhere," Con said, quite sure of that. "Lancho brought something, some relic from somewhere. He drained all the people, all his power relics and the aura from here to do it."

"Then your mate might simply be exhausted," Ashlax proposed.

"I can hope," Con muttered. "Then you can help me. You can draw power from the aura and pass it to her."

"No! Your sister stripped me of power."

Con shook his head. "No, she simply blocked you from using the aura in ritual sorcery. You can still use it passively as the healers do."

Ashlax looked surprised and awed. "Can you teach me?"

Con nodded. "It's simple – Jai taught me." He explained quickly and Ashlax understood.

"And did you teach her too?" Ashlax asked with a faint grin.

"I hope I taught her enough," Con said softly.

"Can you still sense her?" Ashlax asked.

"No, yet I don't think she is dead."

"You don't sound sure."

"I want to be. She made a vow. She promised me that if I did not kill Stacion – she would."

"Perhaps she is exhausted too?" Ashlax considered. "But if Stacion pulled energy from everyone – will she be able to defend herself from him – where ever she is?"

"I think so. Stacion never saw the power in her. He would not know that she could block her mind from him, and I think her power. She showed me how to do that. And I think, I hope, that in that instant before she went, when she pushed you away – she took energy from you. Stacion would not have been able to touch you." Con considered.

"And Bernea, why could she stay?" Ashlax asked.

"Larcia," Con said. "And if she were so injured as to be near death, there would be little energy Stacion could steal, I think too that when you fell on her, you protected her and perhaps some of your energy went to her. However it was – I am grateful."

Ashlax bowed in appreciation of being able to help. "Master, what will you do now?"

"While you care for Bernea, I go and bring warriors and workers here. We must take everything from here. Every scavenger will soon know what happened here and come… I will have litters brought for Bernea and the two dead."

The village was again deserted. No trace of anything Atapi remained. Con had taken all of his people back to his land with the last of the items. Ashlax had supervised the removal of the last items from Stacion's relic caches. All had been drained and the items themselves were either burned or warped or shattered. Even those that Con had been able to make Stacion forget about were useless. He thought perhaps Stacion might have forgotten them, but when he decided to go, he had drained everything at once and only considered them as a group and not individually. Perhaps that was how he had done it. Now, all the shards and wrecked things were buried deep under a pile of rocks.

Con stood in the centre of what once had been the village and let him sense the state of the rest of Stacion's land. It felt dead. The distant trees were burnt; all other vegetation was already turned yellow. The scavenging canines were slinking closer. They sensed the death and decay but they would find nothing here.

He sensed the arrival of another being behind him and turned. He was not surprised to see a young sorcerer.

"Yellonge Tsarnu," Con greeted, recognising the next youngest sorcerer in age to himself. "I was told to expect scavengers."

The sorcerer growled. "I challenge you!"

Con snarled a laugh at him. "Tribeless fool. Look around you. What prestige is there in winning dead land?"

"It would be mine!" the other snarled, creating in an instant, a handful of whirling fire, which he flung at Con.

Con did nothing. In the short distance of twice the other sorcerer's height, the fire ball decreased in size to nothing.

Subsequent ones suffered the same fate. Con merely watched the other's confusion.

"How are you doing that?" Yellonge Tsarnu demanded.

"Actually, I am doing nothing," Con admitted. "For one who was only made a sorcerer in the last ritual – you are poorly prepared for any challenge."

"And you! Who never even performed the ritual! Have you even got a secret name, Con Ansuni?"

"I have my secret name. And I defeated Stacion Ansuni or did your sire not tell you?"

Con spoke calmly. This young sorcerer, without his own tribe, had not been one of those supervising the challenge for succession."

"He said – you won. He said – there is no body," Yellonge Tsarnu snarled.

"No, there is no body. Nor tribe, nor life in these lands. I didn't kill him. The coward fled. I didn't take his knife. By some traditions, this land is no one's land. Your sire gave it to me. This is my victory."

Tsarnu looked around, but he kept one eye on Con. He had heard that the Ansuni line could not be trusted. This had to be a bluff – an illusion.

"Do you accept my challenge – coward?" Yellonge Tsarnu persisted.

"Any challenge would need to be strictly physical," Con told the other. "We could brawl like undisciplined whelps, or fight with swords or knives. If you insist – you may choose which. And if you think that I am still weak from the last battle – I warn you, I am not."

Tsarnu launched another magical attack. Illusions of knives flew at him. The visions became wisps of nothing within feet.

"Yellonge Tsarnu, I do not accept your challenge, and before you again accuse me of cowardice, I will tell you my reasons. Firstly – it is because this would not be an equal match. I am not claiming to be more skilled than you in sorcery – for Larcia would not give a secret name to one who is unworthy."

"Larcia is a myth," Tsarnu snapped.

Con ignored the comment. "Secondly, I am skilled in physical combat. Stacion insisted that I train with his warriors and punished me if I slacked. And thirdly, any power you release to fight me will be sucked up like water into dry ground. More futile demonstrations of sorcery will quickly drain you of energy. Are you ignorant of where your power comes from?"

Tsarnu snarled.

Con continued. "If you were to defeat me you would gain nothing. If I defeated you – I would gain nothing and the Atapi would lose a potential leader who could help strengthen our race."

"I would gain prestige," Tsarnu snarled. "I would have your knife. They gave you your sire's place in the ranking of sorcerers – I'd take that place. I could start a tribe of my own."

"You would need more than that to have outsiders flock to you," Con told him, not intending to reveal to this fool that he himself had his own tribe and land.

"Fight! Coward!" Tsarnu leapt at Con and grabbed for his throat. He also aimed a knee at Con's stomach.

Con reacted instinctively, twisting and grabbing Tsarnu's wrists and flinging him to the ground. In the time it had taken for the leap, Con had Tsarnu pinned to the ground with a dagger at his throat.

"I warned you, Sarax," Con told the defeated sorcerer, as he took the ritual dagger from him. "And I hope that your sire, the Old One has smarter whelps than you and Ashlax. Does he know what you are doing here?"

"No!"

"Then if you wish – we will keep this between us," Con offered. "I do not wish you as an enemy. I would welcome you as an ally. We need wise sorcerers if our race is to survive and thrive. Not foolish ones. If you agree, then when you have your tribe and I have mine – we can support each other and be the stronger for it. Stronger than those old Sorcerers that jealously guard what is theirs and whose tribes are becoming inbred and weak. Are you willing?"

Tsarnu, knowing he was beaten had been expecting a fate like his brother's. He stared at Con, confused. "How do I know I can trust you?"

Con sent a thought to one of his tribe and opened a pass through between himself and his land. Ashlax walked through. Tsarnu's eyes widened in surprise as he took in his brother's appearance.

"You wanted me Master?"

"Please explain to your sibling what our arrangement is?"

Ashlax took in the situation and gave his brother a pitying look.

"I am chief adviser to Con Ansuni," Ashlax said haughtily. "His dam was our elder sister."

"But you are nothing! A slave," Tsarnu growled. But he saw that his brother was clad in garments nothing like a slaves robe. "Stacion Ansuni defeated you!"

"It wasn't Stacion Ansuni," Ashlax told him. "I was defeated, and Con Ansuni has granted me high honour."

"Does Father know? "Tsarnu demanded.

"I dare say he will eventually, but he disowned me, so I no longer have obligations to him."

Tsarnu considered what he had been told. "All right, I agree."

Con let him rise and Tsarnu bowed in respect to the one who had defeated him.

He was surprised when Con returned the courtesy.

"You mock me," Tsarnu accused.

"Not so. It is simply that I would have you as an equal. We are a new generation of sorcerers and we must discover new ways. Would you accept a gift of advice from me?"

Tsarnu nodded warily.

"When you next go to Arkor, think on wanting to know the truth of the Atapi race – and allow the learning to come."

Tsarnu nodded, and decided not to linger any longer. He turned abruptly and 'walked' away.

Con asked Ashlax, "Am I a fool to trust him?"

Ashlax considered. "He's not really a fool, though he probably gave a good demonstration of it. He no doubt thought to try you when you should have been weak. He just didn't know the whole story. My sire wouldn't have revealed everything. He likes secrets too. I, however, would like to know what vision you have had, Con Ansuni."

"Later. I expect that he won't be the last one to come and try me, and I need to find out where Stacion has gone – or he might return to finish me off."

"He left his long knife," Ashlax noted, going over and reaching down for it.

"Leave it on the ground," Con commanded. His voice was calm and controlled.

Ashlax paused in his movement and glanced at Con. His fingers itched to grab the blade. He saw strangers approaching – Kumatan – the enemy.

"Step back from it," Con insisted.

Ashlax finally obeyed. He saw weapons in the hands of the enemy – aimed at him.

Con drew his own knife and threw it on the ground. He stood straight and proud and walked in a completely non- threatening way towards the Kumatan. He stopped a length away from them.

"Traeger. Welcome. I had expected you to take advantage of the dropping of shields to invade my land."

"Your land!" Jenha exclaimed from behind his father.

"Such as it now is," Con agreed. "I shan't be staying. As I said, I had expected you and was waiting."

"Are you challenging me," Traeger Mosellan demanded, arrogantly aloof and suspicious.

"I have no need to challenge you," Con stated. "Nor do I feel the need to dominate or be dominated by you. I was told that once our two races were equal - each with our own role to play."

"So, you challenged your Sire and won – did you kill him?" Traeger Mosellan asked.

"No. He fled – retreated from the ritual combat." Con told him. "I won – he is no longer ranked as a Sorcerer. He is barred from our sacred places and from the aura of Korvu."

Traeger Mosellan looked around. "So, where is your tribe?"

"My tribe – those I stole from Stacion – are safe," Con stated. "Those that were here are gone."

"Gone where?" snapped Traeger. "I have no wish to have Stacion Ansuni loose with no idea where."

"On that point – we agree," Con said flatly. "And were it any other Atapi, I would be branded traitor for betraying anything to you. I don't know where he is. He drained this land to its death, drained all his power relics, all his people. Where ever he went – he took all his tribe with him - including Jai, my womb-mate. Two of his warriors died. I fear for Jai if she is too weak to defend herself. Stacion smelt your presence about her. He promised …" Con broke off and shook his head. "I intend to hunt him – where ever he is on Korvu – I will find him or he will be found. His tribe is at risk of dying, for I doubt that Stacion will care for them. And since he has discovered how much power he can harvest from death and torture… if he is desperate enough he will kill his tribe and I doubt that he will stop there."

Traeger Mosellan growled in quick understanding.

"We will hunt him too. Though we must also guard against others like him." Traeger Mosellan warned.

"Like me?" Con queried.

The Traeger's face twitched with suppressed anger. Years of antagonistic exchanges – with injury done to Kumatan – could not be forgotten easily.

"Yes!" he hissed.

Con bowed his head briefly. "As I said before, I have no wish to be your enemy. I am not like my sire. Most, I can't say all, Atapi sorcerers are not either. I am young – yes – but I have been given the rank my sire lost. I intend to have Stacion Ansuni hunted like the feral beast he is, and to use my new rank to influence my kind to retreat from conflict with those who should be our equals."

Traeger Mosellan's expression didn't change.

Jenha dared to speak. "I believe Con Ansuni."

"What would you know?" Traeger Mosellan snapped.

"Jai Ansuni came to us – offered us a way to find the source of those ghastly murders – done she believed by one of her tribe. Obaki is helping us – sworn to you and to Con Ansuni."

"Very well," Traeger Mosellan decided. "I will limit the other Traeger's to hunting for Stacion Ansuni. But if any of the sorcerers attack Kumatan, I will hold you – Con Ansuni – responsible and I will personally exact vengeance on you."

"Father! That is not fair!" Jenha protested.

"If he isn't big enough for the task – he shouldn't have the position!" Traeger Mosellan snarled.

"Father…"

"It is not a problem," Con spoke to Jenha. "I understand his anger – and share it. I will encourage every un-landed sorcerer to seek Stacion with me. If one of them finds him, kills him, and can bring his ritual knife before the tribal sorcerers – I will give them this land for their own."

Traeger Mosellan stared at Con. "What else are you planning?"

"Only that. With such incentive as their own land, it will distract any young hotheads from challenging Kumatan, and me. And my elders will be too busy ensuring that their tribes are protected from Stacion's anger."

"Father…there is something else," Jenha interrupted. "Jai wanted Lancho found, but she also wanted Obaki to find out what he was talking to traders about."

"And what has this to do with anything?"

"She spoke Atapi to him, just before she was dragged away. She thought it possible that Stacion thought of fleeing from Korvu."

"Impossible," Traeger Mosellan snapped. "Atapi sorcerers are bound to the land. They can't leave. It would take too much energy, power - whatever. The worlds those traders come from are years away in their spaceships."

Jenha tried to speak again but is fathers silenced him with a gesture.

Con suddenly had the need to ask, "Can Kumatan leave Korvu?"

"It is possible – but we have no space going ships."

Con's sudden dreadful thought was not eased. He felt, however, that Traeger Mosellan was in no mood for further argument.

Con briefly met Jenha's eyes and shared a moment of silent accord.

It seemed that Traeger Mosellan had not understood that Stacion Ansuni was no longer bound to the land. Nor that he had taken an incredible amount from his land. If he had even thought that Atapi sorcerers could, like Traegers, cross planes from place to place in moments when others needed days – would he be so sure Stacion was still on Korvu?

Con looked again at the drained dying land around him. It would take many seasons to recover, if it ever did.

"I wish you well, Traeger Mosellan," Con bowed slightly. "I will go to Arkor tonight and seek wisdom there. I will look to see if, in all our history, Atapi have ever left Korvu. Perhaps your son could search your ancient texts for similar knowledge."

Traeger Mosellan nodded, but Jenha looked unimpressed.

"I didn't know that Atapi kept history records." Jenha muttered.

Con forced a semblance of a Kumatan smile onto his face and managed to keep his teeth from showing. "Our history is as ancient as yours, Traeger, and recorded on the Rock of Arkor for any who know how to read it."

Con saw intense interest in the Traeger's eyes. "If Larcia permits, I would be willing to teach your son."

"Larcia is a myth," Traeger Mosellan stated. He looked as if he thought Con would corrupt his son.

"Is she?" Con asked. Then he bowed, took Ashlax by the arm and 'walked' away – back to his tribe. He had much to do there.

Chapter 27

"What do you mean? You can't find that Atapi?" Traeger Mosellan roared. He felt betrayed, tricked.

"He just vanished. We went to where you directed us and he confirmed that an Atapi had been there. He stayed in the wagon. I asked the people about it about the owner. I have a description of the trader and reports on what he was buying and selling. When I went back inside, the Atapi had gone. He could not have gone out the windows and I was never far from the door. There is a guard on the wagon now, but I think the Atapi and our quarry have fled."

"Follow up on what you found," Traeger Mosellan directed. "And find that Atapi. If he can walk out of that wagon without using the door, he must be a sorcerer."

Later, Jenha suggested, "Perhaps Stacion dragged him away like he did to Jai. He swore to you and to Jai, but perhaps he was still bound to Stacion in some way?"

Traeger Mosellan's anger receded. "What makes you say that?"

"Well, Jai didn't want to go and couldn't stop it. I would not think her well disposed towards her Sire…and some things that I read in those really old archives – about the Atapi culture."

"We will discuss that another time. What other ideas do you have?"

"Only that Obaki might be lying somewhere, weak, exhausted and in danger from thieves and robbers."

"Then I will put you in charge of looking for him," Traeger Mosellan told his son.

The Ritual of Ascension, held at the Rock of Arkor, was usually a unifying experience. A sorcerer, newly elevated to a tribal leader, was welcomed by his elders, and educated in his responsibility to the Atapi race as a whole and to his tribe. That it should mean consolidating with other sorcerers in times of trouble was often quickly forgotten again in the current times of diminishing tribe size and resources.

Con had requested that younger sorcerers, as yet without their own lands or tribes, be allowed to participate. They would learn what was expected of them.

After the Old One shared the story of Loschak with them, the Elders ruled that Con had every right to the once shunned land. His by right of defeating Stacion, who had weakened Loschak, so he could not defend his tribe, and by right of inheriting Loschak's knife. Con ensured that all knew of this earlier example of Stacion's unfitness to rule.

Anger rose afresh, and even those sorcerers who were least willing to co-operate with each other – agreed that the ex-sorcerer must be found. Must die.

The Old One spoke words of caution. "The nameless one has learnt that killing gives him power. Killing for just that reason is taboo – even if the victim is an enemy. If he is desperate enough, he may even kill Atapi. Those of us with tribes – must ensure they are safe."

Con spoke up, as permitted by his new rank and by the fact that this was his rite of ascension.

"The land of the nameless one, mine by right – will need much time to recover, but those of us without lands, without tribe – may seek the traitor. If any of you find and kill him, take his knife – I will cede that land to that one."

Con observed the young sorcerers, all older than him, and was pleased with what he saw. They would all regard him with favour and would leave him alone for now. They would leave no trace unsmelt for Stacion Ansuni. Wherever he had gone – if he was on Korvu – one of them would find him.

Con said nothing to the other Atapi about his fear that Stacion had gone to another world. The Kumatan did not think it possible – and the most likely option must be considered first. But Con knew what Stacion had been thinking, and Lancho had brought a relic....

Well, if he was on Korvu – he should be able to reach Jai. If Stacion hadn't killed her. Perhaps she was just exhausted...

Obaki cursed as he woke and found his face in the dust. He was old, unfit and must have drunk too much fermented hare's milk. He had been dreaming he had been locked up.

Then he looked around. He knew where he was, but it was all dead. He couldn't find the strength to move. All he could do was roll over and let the hot sun bake his front as it had his back.

He was free. Free to hunt. Then he recalled the astounding events. He had been a prisoner – but he had a chance to regain his honour. Serving Kumatan and Atapi.

Obaki lifted his arm and saw the unfamiliar pink flesh of the Kumatan. Everything came back to him. Including the terrifying moment when some unseen force had lifted him and sent him flying from the wagon – through the wagon – to here, where it had dropped him.

He had sensed Stacion Ansuni – feared for his life – but the sorcerer had not been thinking about one traitor, but some strange place where Obaki had never been, that had trees that looked wrong.

Obaki stood when he finally felt he could. He began to search the village. He found nothing living, but he read the story in the tracks on the ground. Belatedly he recognised the village and wondered how he had got there and how he would get back to where he had been.

After a time of reaching through his memories, he remembered the stone that Jai had given him. He reached into his pouch – no, Kumatan called them pockets, touched the stone and thought of Jai.

Con felt a tug at his mind and stopped speaking to Ashlax to consider it. At first it had felt like Jai, but it wasn't.

"Continue storing the food, Ashlax. I'm going back to the village," Con told him. He ignored Ashlax's cautioning words.

He walked across planes and arrived in the cover of some dead and brittle bushes. He saw a figure, apparently Kumatan, wondering aimlessly about. Yet something about the gait did not seem right.

"Why are you here, Kumatan?" Con challenged, stalking towards the intruder.

Obaki spun around, dreadfully afraid, but it wasn't Stacion Ansuni who spoke, but a young whelp. A whelp wearing the robes of a sorcerer.

"I am Obaki," was all he felt he could say, until he knew who challenged him. "I am seeking…"

Con stopped him. "I know," he had read the creatures mind. "I am seeking Jai too. Why are you here? Have you found…"

Obaki shook his head.

Con growled softly. "Jai told me of you. I welcome your service. I want you to continue – now that Jai has gone."

"Gone, Master Con?" Obaki asked.

"I have defeated my Sire, but the coward fled, taking all that remained of his tribe with him. Jai too." Con explained.

"I was dragged here," Obaki reported. "I thought he had forgotten me."

"You were lucky," Con told him bluntly. "He had forgotten, but you were still linked to him by way of blood. When he fled, he drained the land, drained his relics, and drained his tribe. Where he has gone is not known and must be discovered as soon as possible. Your task is most important. I have set both Atapi and Kumatan looking for him. If he is on Korvu – he will be found."

"If?" Obaki queried. "Where else could he be?"

"Off our world. On some other world. Just before he vanished, he got a relic off Lancho. An off world relic."

"What was it like, master?" Obaki asked eagerly.

Con described the odd shaped drinking cup.

"Yes! Yes! I heard of something like that but it was expensive. I didn't think Lancho could have bought one."

"Buy it?" Con queried. "You were with the Kumatan too long. Stacion or Lancho would steal it. Do you know the way back?"

Obaki shook his head. He had that Kumatan gesture copied well.

"Never mind. I will get you there." Con decided.

Bernea waited until Con was alone before asking him what was on her mind. Since becoming tribal leader, Con had little freedom, or free time.

"Has there been word about Jai?"

Con reached for her, wanting to feel the calmness she exuded, and sense the new life within her.

"No, nor of Stacion. It is as if they all just vanished."

"Then she must be dead," Bernea slumped.

"I would say that I think she lives, but I have no proof. I just believe that if she'd died, I would have felt it." Con admitted.

"If all the young hot heads have not found Stacion – where could he be?" Bernea asked.

"I have a private fear that he is on some other world. And if that is so, I doubt he will ever return. Nor Jai. But at least we would be rid of him."

"But what if people live there?" Bernea asked. "With no protection against him?"

"I cannot do anything about it. I am now bound to my land and to Korvu."

Bernea accepted his words as truth, but didn't like them. "Who can?"

Con considered the question. There was only one answer.

"If anyone – the Kumatan."

"Then you must warn them. Make them do something," Bernea insisted.

"I tried. They think it is impossible that Stacion is not on Korvu. And they would never take orders from me. They think us barbarians."

"Didn't you say that they and us should be equals?" Bernea reminded him.

"Convince them of that," Con muttered. "Still, it has been only one moon cycle. Stacion could still be licking his wounded pride."

Chapter 28

Traeger Mosellan received a summons from Karravin, the leader of the Kimh. This in itself wasn't unusual; the Kimh had been very concerned about finding the renegade sorcerer Stacion Ansuni.

What was unexpected was the timing of the request since had had given his latest report only the previous day.

Jenha Mosellan sensed his father's annoyance. He said nothing, but wondered what was afoot. He'd heard that the other Traegers were getting tired of looking for someone who obviously didn't want to be found. It had been months now and no Atapi atrocities had occurred since Stacion's disappearance.

Some Traegers were convinced he was dead, or at least was no longer a threat. Jenha agreed with his father, he wanted to be sure. He feared an angry and vengeful Stacion Ansuni.

Would the Kimh Council – the rulers of Korvu – call off the hunt? They would be foolish to do so. Old Karravin, currently the leader, listened to his advisers, mostly Kimh who were dreamers or philosophers, and to the Traegers – the highest ranking Kumatan. What if all the other Traegers wanted to stop searching?

Not long after his father left, Jenha Mosellan heard a commotion at the door of the suite. He saw Obaki scuttle in past the servant. He was acting oddly, almost excited.

"What is it?" Jenha asked, jumping up.

"Not here, young master," Obaki shrugged a shoulder towards the servant. Jenha dismissed the woman.

"Now what…" Jenha began, only to be interrupted by Obaki.

"The trader's, the ones I have been looking for, are back," he began. "That relic, the 'chalice' they called it, came from a planet the people there call Earth. It's actually an interdicted planet. The traders are not meant to go there because the people are savages still. They don't know other worlds exist. But these traders – well – they snuck in. They say that relics from such places are very valuable because they are rare."

Jenha felt a surge of alarm. "Did they see any Atapi there?"

"No – you misunderstand. They haven't been back. Their consortium punished them for going there. And now, they won't. But they recognised the description and remembered the 'chalice' being stolen. I must tell master Con about this."

"I will see that he learns of it – but there is nothing he can do. He is bound to Korvu now that he is a tribal sorcerer. He can't leave – and shouldn't."

Suzi, Jenha's sister, trotted into the suite and came to Jenha. "The Kimh are buzzing like flies. My friend, Kimi, heard her father being told that traders saw lizards – I mean Atapi – on some world they went to. The traders were angry because some of their number were killed by them. They are demanding retribution."

Obaki uttered a Kumatan expletive. "I may serve the Kumatan, but I do not grant them mastery over us. The traders should approach us!"

"Easy there, Obaki," Jenha spoke calmly. "Your people keep to themselves. The traders may have met some of you in unfavourable circumstances. Meaning no offence, but most of them refer to your people as lizards. And because you don't look like them – think you aren't worth knowing. And again, intending no offense, we, the Kumatan, particularly the Traegers, are responsible for seeing that your sorcerers don't become like Stacion."

"You couldn't stop that one!" Obaki snarled. "I've heard what he's done and if your Slavemaster – Traegers hadn't been so interfering, our sorcerers would have muzzled him."

"Let's not argue, my friend," Jenha said quietly. "In this instance, if what Suzi heard is right, we must do something. Your sorcerers can't leave here, we can."

Obaki collapsed onto the floor.

"What's the matter, Obaki?" Suzi asked, concerned. She had grown to like the short tubby Atapi.

"What will the Traegers do if they go there? Kill all of us?"

Jenha started. "Father wouldn't..."

"Others might," Obaki wailed. "Then what will happen to Mistress Jai?"

Suzi went stiff. "She might be dead already."

"When I spoke to Con Ansuni, he believed she lived, even though he couldn't reach her mind. Con thinks that even though he threatened her with death for consorting with you, he will need her skills more than ever on a world where he cannot draw on the aura. Master Con believed they'd gone off Korvu, even though Master Traeger did not."

Jenha sighed. "I don't think they wanted to believe it. I shudder to think of people with no defences against Stacion Ansuni, but many would only care that he was not here. Come, Obaki – I think we should go quickly to Con Ansuni. Suzi – can you keep Father busy until I get back?"

Suzi nodded and sat down in a chair to await news.

Jenha returned to hear a loud argument between Suzi and his father.

"Father, if you must go, so will I. I'm no wilting court flower, like the Kimh girls. I am your daughter. I am one from an ancient line of Traegers. I can help you. Jai is my friend. I want to help her. I want to help my father and brother."

"Suzelaine," Mosellan snapped at his daughter. "You will be a danger to yourself. I will have to have someone guarding you. You will stay here."

"No! Father, you insist on thinking me weak — like mother — I'm not. You insist on being blind to the fact that I've got as much power as Jenha…"

"Women cannot be Traegers," Mosellan snapped.

"Who said I wanted to be? But I can do what Jenha does!"

Jenha looked and saw his sister walk three steps forward, vanish, and reappear across the room. "I could do more if you would open your eyes and teach me."

"Father, what is going on?" Jenha interrupted the argument.

Traeger Mosellan exhaled his breath slowly, getting control of his temper.

"The trader consortium has found an Atapi colony on another planet. They came here and demanded we do something about them. The High Minister of the Kimh has granted me the honour of being allowed to finish the job I started."

"It sounds more like they think you deliberately let him escape," Suzi said, annoyed at what she perceived as a slight on his honour and competence.

"When father told the council what Con believed," Jenha told his sister, "They all said such a thing was impossible, that Stacion had to still be on Korvu. Father — how soon do we leave?"

"I must make plans," Jellarn said. "We will be on our own, on a strange planet. We must be self-sufficient for however long we need to be there. The traders are willing to take a small team down to the surface. No doubt it is so they have a legal reason to go where their kind should never have gone in the first place. I don't even know what these 'Earth humans' look like. The traders say they look much like us but how can that help when they think Kimh and Kumatan are alike."

"I will help you, Father," Suzi offered. "I can write down ideas of what domestic support staff you might need and supplies. Jenha can help you with the rest."

Jellarn Mosellan looked carefully at his daughter. "Thank you – I had not thought of household staff. Perhaps you could also suggest people who can tolerate rough living and are also able to fight if needed to."

"Count me in for one," Suzi offered again.

"I do not want to risk you, Suzelaine. Your mother would never forgive me if Stacion found you and recognised you."

"Mother is no longer around and Stacion Ansuni would never expect me to be on that Earth place. And I think I could find Jai Ansuni more easily than you men."

"Before I agree," Jellarn said sternly. "I will test you to see how much you have learnt behind my back."

Suzi blushed scarlet. Jenha winked at her.

"And you, my son," Jellarn spun around and glared at Jenha, "Will go back to the archives and look for any mention of Kumatan leaving Korvu and for any mention of ways we can hide our settlement from the prying eyes of 'Earth humans'."

Jenha groaned. He had only just finished looking for indications of the ancient Atapi culture.

"Yes, Father," he said meekly. "Who else will be going?"

Jenha wondered why his father still seemed so angry.

"Katech will be the mission overseer – Supreme Leader – and Traeger Nascen will be under me."

"Don't they trust you," Suzi muttered. "Inki Nascen says his father should have your place in the council."

"Nascen is experienced and competent," Jellarn said, calming himself. "I could have worse…"

"You do," Jenha muttered. "Katech. A right twit and would love to see you fail."

"Jenha!"

"It's true. He is jealous because he didn't inherit the Traeger abilities, and his bloodline isn't as ancient as ours. He will be at you to make sure that I am trained properly. As if I am not."

"I will expect you to be elevated before we leave. That means, my son that you will also need to do a lot of study. If you pass the Traeger testing before we leave, he will have no say in anything about you."

"Then I will study very, very hard," Jenha promised.

"It will be your understanding of the Nuath that is most important, since we will be mingling with aliens."

"Isn't it fortunate, Father, that since you made us live in the palace - I have had a lot of time to learn how the Kimh think," Jenha smiled. "I will get started in the archives."

Jenha trotted towards the door of his father's suite. He turned in the doorway and shrugged at Suzi. She walked that way.

"I'm going back to see Con," he whispered to her. "I want to see if he will take me to the Rock of Arkor, or seek there for me on this matter of hiding our settlement. One thing that I learnt in our archives is that Atapi and Kumatan were once equals. Our powers come from the same source. Do you know that a lot of what Atapi sorcerers can do – we can too?"

"What" Suzi exclaimed in a whisper.

"And the more I know about Atapi sorcery, the better I will be able to help find Stacion."

'No, I can't take you there," Con said with some regret. "It would not be safe for you, or wise for me. I am still too new as a sorcerer to be so …daring."

Jenha, squatting opposite Con in the deserted and dead village, shrugged.

"Have you ever heard of anything like what I asked?"

"No, but I am no older that you," Con admitted. "Let me think."

Jenha looked around as he waited. The young sorcerers shadow was standing - not too close – but was watchful and alert.

"All I can think of," Con ventured finally, "Is the writing at the Rock of Arkor. If you went there – you wouldn't see it. I go there, expecting to see it and do."

Con called Ashlax over and asked him the question.

The older Atapi added a similar tale. "My sire keeps his relics in a cave, but I sneaked in once and there was nothing there. My brother asked once but all he was told was that his relics were there in the cave, but in a place where no one was."

Jenha thought on the words. "I don't know if that helps or not, but thanks for coming."

After Jenha had gone, Ashlax sidled closer to Con.

"So it is sure that Stacion has gone. Will you tell the Elders?"

"It would be worth it to know if your Sire thinks it possible," Con decided. "And hope he doesn't spread it, for I would rather the landless sorcerers stayed busy until our entire world has been scoured for him. Though the idea Jenha proposes frightens me. If Stacion is still here, but hidden…"

"We'd know," Ashlax decided. "That one might lick his wounds for a time but one tribe would not be enough for him. He'd come back and torment the Kumatan – or you. Except that he doesn't know where you are now."

"He might figure it out," Con countered, thinking of the nightmare creatures he'd made illusions of. Unless Stacion thought he had used the simpler 'nightmare chant' that freed a person's individual demons.

"He can't be so powerful anymore," Ashlax proposed. "If he returns, you can fight him. But I think he is gone and I don't envy the Kumatan the task of searching a whole world for him."

"Nor do I envy Jai the task I failed to finish," Con admitted.

Epilogue

The trader ship observed the planet from a long way out.

"What is happening down there," Katech demanded. He could see indications of explosions.

"Some kind of war," the trader leader shrugged. "I've seen worse. This war is mostly in that one area."

"And what location did that relic come from," Traeger Nascen asked.

"That same area," the trader shrugged again. "Or so the renegades told me."

Nascen glanced at Mosellan. "Stacion's work?"

"War is not unusual in pre-space faring cultures, Nascen, but I would not discount Stacion being attracted to war or to abet it. Think of the power all the deaths bring to one with no moral scruples."

"Trader, can you get us down without being noticed?" Katech asked.

"Of course," the trader claimed. "Though once down you will be on your own. You will have to call us if you want to leave. Have you the means to call us?"

"Of course," Nascen assured him. "We have all the skills we need, and being able to keep in touch with Korvu is one."

Jenha overheard the comment and kept his face impassive. Such means of communication would need to be constructed from local materials. Half their small group were technologists. None of the group had family ties back on Korvu. In case they didn't return. Though once the initial group had settled, more guards and others could be brought to Earth. But the traders did not have to know the full details. This assignment was not going to be easy.

One thing was a relief to all. The people of the world below were basically similar to Kumatan. Large proportions were pale skinned. All had two legs and two arms and so on. But their skin tones did vary a lot and so did hair colour. The Kumatan should not look as alien as the Atapi.

Jenha stifled the excitement he felt at being a part of this assignment to an alien world. It was a vital task, and it would be hard work, getting settled, blending in, learning the local culture. It would bring honour when the succeeded. Even having to take lessons from Nascen and Katech couldn't change how he felt.

Stacion Ansuni had better watch out. His freedom and life were limited.

The End

If you enjoyed
Korvu – The Beginning

I hope you would consider writing a review and
placing it on the website of your book supplier.

Discover Other Titles by Margaret Gregory

NOVELS

THE WILD ONE

Sixteen year old Jai Cassidy thought she was finally free of her family until
she is discovered by her other relatives…the ones that aren't human. Jai
uses her natural perversity and cunning to escape their control, but
catapults herself into the middle of a deadly feud between two alien races.

ATAPI SORCERESS
The sequel to The Wild One

Jai Cassidy is beginning her mission of reversing the decline of the non-
humanoid Atapi. As a sorceress and an Atapi-Human hybrid, she is
vehemently disliked by the male Atapi sorcerers and the humanoid rulers
of Korvu. Her task is complicated by the treachery of a group of alien
engineers, who are inciting insurrection and harsh reprisals.

The Tymorean Trust Book 1 - POWER RISING

The Tymorean Trust - When peace rules Tymorea - Peace reigns in the
universe.
Chosen to be the Advocates of the mystical and incorporeal Guardians of
Peace, twins Tymos and Kryslie must first learn to control and use the
power rising in them - or it will destroy them.
On Tymorea, only the ruling Triumvirate Governors are powerful enough
to guide the strong-willed alien-bred twins until they have mastered their
power.

The Tymorean Trust Book 2 - GREAT ONES

The peace of the Guardian Planet, Tymorea, is in deadly peril. War there will create ripples of unrest and destruction throughout the settled universe.
Tymos and Kryslie, still adolescents, have barely mastered their power and Llaimos is still less than a year old, but they are the three chosen to be Advocates of the mystical Guardians of Peace, to safeguard the Tymorean Trust.

The Tymorean Trust Book 3 - THE RETURN TO EARTH

Even before the war on Tymorea, the Elders foresaw that Great Ones Tymos and Kryslie would have an imperative mission on Earth.
But as the Tymoreans prepare to build an Earthbase to support them, they discover that specifications for two vital protective shields are missing.
Now, nearly a century later, Tymos and Kryslie must find his work and build the generator before the base is found.

The Tymorean Trust Book 4 - EARTH MISSION

Just before their graduation from the prestigious WSRA Washington University, Tymos and Kryslie Ward deliberately disappear.
The Great Ones have foreseen the capture and death of the new Tymorean missionaries and discovered that the leader of the Eastern Imperium plans to undermine the United World Nations.
Tymos and Kryslie must protect their kin and prevent a potentially devastating world war.

The Tymorean Trust Book 5 – ALIEN CONTACT

Tymos and Kryslie Ward, hide their Tymorean intelligence and abilities while working as low ranked technicians at the WSRA's lunar base. When an alien ship arrives at Lunar One, pursued by a powerful enemy who will stop at nothing to get what he wants, only the two Tymorean Great Ones have the knowledge and abilities to overcome him, but to do so they must risk their sanity, and their souls.

If she was going to die young, like her mother, Gwen Willard was determined to die rich and she had very few years to do it. Her first step was to leave home. She met Hooch, who taught her some exciting and illegal skills. She was the Dracos lucky mascot until she came to the attention of the police.

Then her uncanny knack for predicting trouble, warned her to flee to the city and change her name.

Life wasn't easy. She was 15, had little money and no regular job, but her new skills came in handy. Then she crossed the path of an evil and unscrupulous man and she didn't want him to have his way.

WANDA: CHOOSING CRIME

Wanda was free. She was never going back to jail. But she was homeless, almost penniless and Harrison Franklin had a long and vengeful memory. Jim Phillips had a long memory too, and Wanda had saved his life. Could he save her from Franklin?

SHORT STORIES:

GRAFFITI GIRL

Valerie has become known as "The Graffiti Girl" but she is more than just a street artist.
She sees and paints life her way.

In Valkyrie, the second story, Valerie, blinded by an explosion, must learn to paint and see again.

GHOST WRITER

Edwina is a ghost with a mission - to find out why she died.
Only to do so, she must first help another girl.

Connect to Margaret Gregory

My Smashwords author profile:
https://www.smashwords.com/profile/view/msgdragon

Connect with me on LinkedIn:
http://au.linkedin.com/pub/margaret-gregory/72/a36/186/

Friend me on Facebook:
http://www.facebook.com/margaret.gregory.399